THE ALIEN'S BACK!

GRACE KENSINGTON

1

———

Maxim felt like the breath was caught in his lungs. It was as though he couldn't bring it all the way in, but he also couldn't let it all of the way out. It swelled in his chest, amplifying the pounding of his heart until it felt as though each beat was shaking the blood in his veins and reverberating in his ears. Ahead of him he could see his father caught in the clash of the battle. It had been so many years since he had seen Aegeus, but Maxim knew his face and the way that he moved. He had watched him for the first years of his life and could remember every detail of him, from the way that he looked when he went into the kitchen to greet Ellora first thing in the morning, to the stern look on his face and the tightness in his shoulders when he left the house and marched to battle. He remembered him with his mind and carried him in his heart, and he would always have been able to recognize him. Maxim had known who Aegeus was from the moment that he saw him running toward the battle, his sword blazing.

Now Maxim was watching him, his eyes locked on him,

but he was unable to get to him. Aegeus was on the other side of the battle, his feet moving rapidly beneath him as his hands cut through the air, swinging his weapon. He fought with an intensity that was breathtaking, showing that nothing that he had been through in the years that he had been away from the Mikana kingdom and from Uoria itself had taken the fire from his soul and the power from his presence. Maxim could see the father that he had adored and admired when he was a child even behind the weathered face and the body that was still large, but seemed somehow diminished. He wondered if that was only his perception because he himself was larger now that he was an adult, or if Aegeus truly was smaller now.

The battle continued to rage around him and Maxim felt pushed back away from his father by the violent clash occurring to either side. No matter how much he struggled to get closer to him, the fighting of the two armies acted as a wall in between them, preventing him from getting any closer to Aegeus. Maxim didn't even know if his father had seen him. Though he felt as though there had been a fleeting glance when Aegeus had looked at him before the first slash of his sword into the body of one of the hybrids, his father had made no indication that he had seen him, or that if he did, that he knew who Maxim was. It was somewhat sad to think that his father had spent so many years away from him that he wouldn't know who Maxim was, but it was something that he couldn't change, that he couldn't blame his father for. A sobering thought settled into Maxim's mind and caused him to take a step back, further distancing himself from Aegeus.

Perhaps his father had seen him. Perhaps when he was running toward him across the desert surface of Penthos, his eyes had locked on Maxim the same way that Maxim's had locked on him, but he didn't have the same reaction. Instead of being thrilled the way that Maxim was, perhaps Aegeus felt distanced, that he didn't want to be near his son. Or even worse, perhaps he didn't feel anything at all.

The sound of a strangled cry behind him broke Maxim free of his thoughts and he turned to see George collapse to the ground. The human man's hands went to his throat and he clawed at it as if he were trying to pull away something that was threatening to choke him. His feet dug into the sand as he pushed away from the unseen force, struggling against it in an effort to free himself from something that he couldn't see, but could obviously feel. Maxim looked ahead of the scientist and saw one of the hooded creatures standing in front of him, one gloved hand held out like he was choking George. Maxim realized that the man was controlling George with nothing more than the force of his mind, a terrifying capability that brought a new level of intensity to the fight.

Maxim was starting to take a step toward the hooded creature when he saw Azra step up behind it and plunge his sword into the creature's back. The pain seemed to break its concentration, enabling George to scramble to his feet. Azra slashed away the creature's hood, allowing it to fall away and reveal a face that was nothing short of gruesome. Half looked cold and slimy while the other half appeared to be covered in a thick, black shield that stretched across the bottom of its face, concealing its lips so that it looked as though he didn't have a mouth at all. The creature turned toward Maxim as if feeling his eyes on him and surged toward him, his hand held out toward Maxim's throat. He felt the first hints of tightening that was starting to stop his breath. Remembering what he had seen George going through, Maxim dropped down to the ground and rolled out of the way so that he was no longer in the line of control of the hooded creature. He immediately felt the tightening diminish and reached forward to slash at the creature's legs with his blade. The creature tumbled to the ground, his legs no longer able to support his body.

The creature pulled itself up so that it was on its hands and knees, then lifted its head to look at Maxim. He could see the pain and the anger in its eyes, its jaw set fiercely.

"You will not win," the creature growled at him.

It spoke to him in a voice that seemed to reach down into Maxim and create a dark ember burning in his soul, as if the creature itself hadn't really spoken to Maxim, but that something harbored within it had spoken to something deep within Maxim. He slid his hand down his sword to shorten the blade, ignoring the pain as the sharp edge cut down into palm and fingers. In one swift motion he brought the blade up so that the pointed tip dug into the soft underside of the hybrid's chin. For a moment there was no reaction and then the creature looked into his eyes, the gaze burning into his as though he didn't want Maxim to ever forget what it looked like to have the life slip out of him.

Maxim held his grip, not relenting even as the creature began to gasp and gurgling sounds came from its throat. Finally it slumped, its body falling to the ground, and Maxim pulled his blade away. He was climbing to his feet when he heard a scream ripple through the battlefield toward him. For a moment he thought that someone had seen his actions and was horrified by his brutality, but as he looked up he realized that not only was what he did far from the most brutal action that was occurring on that field, but it was also not the cause for the scream that was now being repeated through the crowd. At the edge of the battlefield he saw a massive animal coming toward them. Its body was larger than anything that he had ever seen and the strength of its muscles was obvious from the way that it moved.

Fear tightened throughout him and Maxim felt the compulsion to join the others who were now starting to run from the animal. The longer that he looked at it, the more familiar it seemed. A description of it seemed to formulate in his mind and he realized that this was something that had been described in the papers he found in the compound. A thought rose in the back of his mind, telling him that this was the creature that had attacked Kyven and Emerie when they were in the quarry, leaving his brother with the horrifying injuries that had made it necessary for him to go back to Uoria with the ship.

He scooped up his sword and started toward the animal, determined to avenge the pain and suffering that his brother had suffered at the wrath of the animal. He had been so focused on the animal's huge head and wide, lumbering stride that he hadn't paid attention to its back. As he neared it, however, he noticed the dark figure sitting astride its tremendous shoulders. The sight brought him to a stop and he stared up at the figure, narrowing his eyes to try to see who it was. He didn't recognize it, but could soon tell that it was a woman. She didn't look like any of the women who he knew from Uoria and he wondered if she might be a member of the hybrid army, though she wasn't wearing the thick hooded robe that set them apart from those fighting on the other side.

Beside the animal he saw a man walking alongside it, his hand occasionally brushing through the thick fur of its leg. Though the man was wrapped tightly in a bandage, he didn't appear to be frightened or as though he were being forced to walk along with it. Around him, Maxim could see the hybrids scrambling backwards away from the animal, telling him that they knew what it was. This was the Meldor, the animal that seemed mythical when Maxim read about it but now knew was what attacked Kyven and Emerie. The hybrids knew about it and understood the power that it had, and many were obviously too terrified to even consider staying on the battlefield to face it. This meant that the animal, and therefore the woman on its back and the man walking alongside it, were not members of their forces and instead were there to fight on his side. As he watched, he saw that the hybrids were leaving behind the members of Maxim and Pyra's army that they had wounded, and that the Denynso warriors were rushing to rescue them.

Maxim returned his weapon to its sheath and rushed toward the nearest wounded man, helping pull him up off of the ground. He heard the woman on the back of the animal call down to Azra, reassuring Maxim that this was a woman he could trust. She instructed the men to put the wounded on the back of the Meldor and Maxim complied, helping to hoist men onto the animal's back until they couldn't fit any more. He watched as the animal took off in the direction of the compound and then turned back to those still on the battlefield. The battle had greatly thinned, but those who had not dissipated seemed to be fighting with even greater intensity, as if the presence of the Meldor and the loss of the wounded had somehow reinforced their efforts and forced them into harder service. He scanned the field for his father, but couldn't see him. Around him some of the rest were started off of the field toward the compound, following the tremendous footsteps of the Meldor, while hybrids rushed away in other directions.

Maxim knew that he could have gone along with them, followed them to the compound and started the process of recovering from the battle and reconnecting with those who had come from Earth. But he knew that the battle wasn't truly over yet. He couldn't return to the compound until the conflict was over. No matter what happened, he couldn't abandon the battle until it was completely at an end. Not even for a moment would he allow the hybrids to think that they had bested him, that he was retreating from them. He would never run. He would never give up. Until the last moment, he would stay and fight.

2

Severine's mind was spinning as she tapped her heels into the Meldor's side to urge it to move faster toward the compound. She was stunned at how extreme the reaction to the animal had been by nearly everyone who was on the battlefield. When she decided to bring the animal up out of the tunnels for what was like the first time in many, many years, she would have thought that it would have been the animal itself that would have had the most severe reaction to being on the surface of the planet again rather than making its way through the deep darkness of the tunnels. This was an animal that was intelligent and thoughtful, making its captivity underground even more painful for her to think about. She knew that it understood what was happening to it and had the capacity in its mind and heart to long for the light that it remembered from when it was young and the feeling of companionship, even if it came from a different species. She knew that the animal would be miserable always being surrounded by darkness and that it would want light, but also knew that it would cause it pain if it did have it. This created an existence of emptiness and tension, torn between the existence that it knew that it could have had, and the one that was forced on it.

The Meldor, however, had reacted far better to being out of the tunnels than she would have expected. It had hesitated as she guided it toward an exit that had a gentler incline, allowing it to walk up out of the ground, but she had spoken to it softly and gently, encouraging it to go along with them. Finally it seemed to have given its trust over to her and allowed her to guide it up out of the ground and into the diminishing light of the day. It was when they approached the battlefield that she witnessed the intense reaction, but from a source that surprised her. The hybrids had been visibly afraid when they had seen the animal. Many had backed away from the fight and run from the animal, putting themselves in severe risk of being captured by the Valdicians and being put through repro-gramming. Their training had taught them never to leave a fight until they had gone through all of their planned maneuvers for that attack. She could already tell by the way that the hybrids had run from the battle that they weren't finished with their maneuvers, but were simply retreating.

It would have made sense to her for the army of Denynso, Eteri, Irisa, humans, and Mikana to be startled when they saw the animal. It was something that none of them would have encountered before and they wouldn't have known what to expect from it. This was a creature that only existed on Penthos now, though it had once thrived on another planet, and because it had been cast beneath the ground so long before it was unlikely that any of the species, even those that had been on Penthos before, had even heard of this being. To see something this large and visibly fierce would be unnerving for even the fiercest of the warriors. The reaction of the hybrids, though, was far more severe.

This didn't make sense to her. She had been through the training of the hybrid army on Penthos. She knew the hybrids were aware of the existence of the Meldor. Even those who had not been made privy to the sections of the tunnels that were now abandoned knew that the animal was beneath the quarry. They were told that this powerful animal was a weapon. They understood the danger that it posed to their enemies. But they shouldn't have feared it for themselves. It shouldn't have been so incredibly horrifying to them that they would leave their posts in the battle without regard for the goals that had been set out for them, set by the rhythm of the drums.

Suddenly it occurred to her. That was her training. That was what she had gone through in the time that she had spent on Penthos before Ryan transferred her back to Earth and prepared her to fight there. That had been long enough ago that things may not be the same. Things might have changed. The only explanation for the way that the hybrids reacted to seeing the Meldor come toward the battlefield was that their training was different now that it had been when she was on Penthos. Instead of them thinking of this animal as a weapon that could be used to prevent the enemy from coming down into the tunnels and the bunkers that they contained, they thought of it as a threat. Rather than a source of protection, it was now a danger to them, something hanging over their heads to remind them every moment that they did not belong to themselves, but to Ryan and the bend of his whims. The change didn't seem to make sense. Severine couldn't understand why Ryan would shift the focus of that creature and the extensive, deep training that dug inside each of the people brought to Penthos and wired them to do just as Ryan wanted.

The baby on Severine's chest whimpered and she lifted one hand away from the Meldor's fur to pat his back gently, soothing him.

"We'll be there soon," she whispered to him. "We'll be there soon and we won't have to travel anymore tonight. You can have something to eat and sleep without being strapped to me." She took a breath and latched onto the thick dark fur again, leaning down to kiss the top of the baby's head. "I'm sorry that this is the way that your first few days have been. You deserve more to the start of your life than this."

There was a groan from behind her and Severine looked back over her shoulder to see one of the wounded men trying to lift his head from where it had been resting on the Meldor's powerful side.

"Rest," she said. "If you move too much you might fall. We'll be to the compound soon. They'll be able to take care of you there."

Tapping her heels slightly again, she hoped to push the Meldor a little faster, though its huge size told her that it was likely this animal wasn't able to move at a much higher speed that it already was. She wanted to get to the compound as quickly as she could so that these men could get to the healers. Ahead of her she saw the dark outline of the wall surrounding the compound. She had never been allowed beyond the barrier that kept this section of the planet set aside for Ryan when he was on the planet with them and the Valdicians that did his bidding when he wasn't. She only knew that it was within the protection of that wall that he lived and planned their training. The massive gate was standing open and she headed toward it, stopping the Meldor just in front of it. The warriors who had run along with them appeared around them a few moments later and started to help the wounded off of the Meldor's back. She watched as they carried the men into the compound and when they were gone, she encouraged the animal forward again, finally entering the compound.

Ahead of her she saw what looked like a human woman. She was staring at the Meldor with fear in her eyes.

"You don't have to be afraid," Severine told her softly, hoping to calm her enough that she wouldn't incite the instincts within the animal that Severine knew were still there but hoped would not emerge again.

The woman looked up at her.

"Is this thing safe?" she called back.

Severine patted the animal's flank and it stopped walking again. She reached behind her back and released the fabric that held the baby close to her chest. Untying it carefully, she loosened the baby until he rested into her arm, then leaned down and carefully handed the baby to Rilex. Once the baby was safe, she swung her legs over to the side and carefully climbed down until she could jump to the sand in front of the woman.

"This is a Meldor," she told her. "I can assure you that it is perfectly safe."

"And who are you?" the human woman asked.

There was a hint of protective aggressiveness in her voice, but Severine wasn't intimidated. If this woman was already inside the compound it meant that she was one of the round that had been on Penthos while the rest were on Earth. She had a close connection with these people and would want to do what she could to ensure that threats were kept away from them.

"My name is Severine," Severine said. "This is my mate, Rilex." She gestured toward Rilex, now cradling the baby to his chest and murmuring against his soft skin. "I have the trust of those who were on Earth. You can trust me. And you can trust the Meldor. It is just an animal. All it needs is to be taken care of, just like the men. Food, water, and rest. That's all."

The human woman looked at the animal again and its head turned toward her. Severine could see the shift in the woman's eyes as she looked at the Meldor, and she knew that this woman could see the vulnerability in it. She turned back to Severine and nodded.

"Alright," the woman said, gesturing to the cluster of buildings on the other side of the compound. "We aren't using those buildings. They might have some things left in them, but they should be mostly empty. There is one that has double doors nearly the size of one wall, like it might have once been a barn or a stable. If it fits inside, it will be safe there. Bring it there and I'll bring some water."

"Thank you," Severine said.

She rested her hand on the front of the Meldor's neck and guided it toward the buildings that the woman had pointed out to her. She quickly found the one that she had described and pushed aside the double doors to reveal a massive open room. She didn't know what it might have once housed, though she didn't think that it was the barn or stable that the human woman had guessed. Ryan and the Valdicians would have no need for domesticated animals that they would need to house in this size of a building. It had to have some purpose at one time, but Severine didn't know what that purpose could be.

The human woman entered the building a few moments later carrying what looked like a bundled blanket under one arm and a large bucket in her hands. She rested the bucket on the floor several feet in front of the Meldor and Severine saw that it contained the water that the woman had said she would get for the animal. The woman stepped back and crouched down to put the blanket on the floor in front of her. Spreading it out, she revealed a pile of food that she had wrapped inside. Taking part of it, she held it out to Severine.

"Thank you," Severine said, taking the food from the woman's hand.

The woman nodded and tugged the corner of the blanket to draw the rest of the food up close to the bucket so that the Meldor could eat it.

"I didn't know what it would eat," she admitted.

The Meldor walked toward the bucket and dipped its head inside, drinking nearly the entire amount of water before lifting its head again and turning toward the food.

"It seems that it likes it," Severine said, her heart warming at the sight of the animal eating the food that the woman had brought for it. "I appreciate your help..." she hesitated and the woman looked toward her.

"Elise," she said. "My name is Elise."

"Hello, Elise," Severine said.

She could see the nervousness in Elise's eyes when she looked at her and Severine knew that she could recognize that she was a hybrid. She didn't know what to say to her to calm her fears and she knew that this was something that she was going to encounter well into the future, but this was not the time for her to confront it. At this moment all she wanted to do was pretend that the reaction wasn't happening and move forward.

"Do you know Azra?" Elise asked.

Severine shook her head.

"I do," she replied, remembering the warrior from the brief time in the basement. "How do you know him?"

Elise sighed and gazed out of the one of the double doors that was still standing open.

"He's my mate," she explained. "I haven't seen him since my shuttle brought him to Earth with Pyra and the rest. I've been so worried about him."

"I haven't known him for long," Severine said, "but what I have known of him, he is strong and well. He should be here very soon."

3

The battle had erupted into chaos. People ran past Maxim, seeming to not even notice that he was there as they left the battlefield. They were running in different directions, some backtracking and going the other way as if not knowing where they should go or what they should do next. There was a sense of terror in the air around him and the panic seemed to have shattered all of the structured, rhythmic control that the hybrids had when they marched into battle. Maxim stood in the center of the field, looking around himself frantically to try to find Aegeus. He had lost sight of him in the frantic reaction to the Meldor and hadn't seen him since. He worried that he might be one of the men who had been swept off of the ground, too injured to walk, to bring back to the compound for treatment.

Maxim spun around, rushing a few steps in each direction as his eyes took in each of the faces that he saw. Some he recognized, even if their names didn't immediately come to his mind, and those that he didn't know he could link to their side of the army by the way that they were dressed or who they were interacting with, helping him to decipher what was left of the quickly dissipating battle. Finally, he saw Aegeus across the field from him. His father turned toward him and their eyes met for the first time. Even from the distance, he could see the flicker of recognition, the slight change in the older man's face that told Maxim that, at least for that moment, he knew that he was looking into a face that he had seen before. Maxim tried to take a step toward him, but before he was able to say anything or even reach out to him, his vision was obliterated by a surge of flame that seemed to burst up in front of him.

The heat of the flame caused Maxim to take a step back and he raised his hand up to block the glare from his eyes. He had been so startled by the sudden flames that he hadn't processed the scream that was pouring out of it. It cut through the clamor of the melee around him now, slicing through the thick air so that it rang in his ears. Maxim forced himself closer to the flames that were now creating what seemed like a wall across the battlefield and realized that it was made by three people, their bodies engulfed in flames as the ran frantically back and forth across the desert sand. Maxim's stomach turned and he felt horror rush up in his chest. He turned around desperately and rushed to the nearest warrior, one of the very few that were left on the battlefield.

"We have to help them!" he said.

"What do we do?"

Maxim dropped his sword to the ground and began to pull off his shirt. The warrior mirrored his action and soon the men around them were doing the same. Maxim took the small pouch of water that he had on his hip and doused his shirt, the sprinkled more on his body. Bracing himself against the heat, he ran toward the flaming figure in the center of the wall. He dove toward him and felt the flames licking at his skin as he passed through the fire. Soon his hands hit the man and the shirt that he held out covered part of his skin. The force of his body forced the man out of the row of fire and onto the ground. Maxim covered as much of him as he could with his shirt and started forcing him to roll, scooping up sand and burying him in it to suffocate the flames.

On either side of him he could see that the other men were doing the same. One of the warriors came to his side and started using his own shirt to continue dampening the flames on the man that Maxim had brought to the ground. His skin was still stinging from passing through the fire but the intense heat had begun to dissipate and he could no longer see the bright light from the corners of his eyes, telling him that the wall of flame was no longer there. He looked to either side of him and saw that the other men were on the ground, rolling and digging down into the sand to try to put out the remaining flames.

Finally there were no more flames on the man and Maxim carefully turned him over to see his face. He worried that he hadn't gotten to him fast enough, that even with the effort that he had put forth to save him, that the flames were too intense, too quickly and he didn't survive. Relief washed over him when he saw the man grimace as grains of sand fell away from his face. It was an expression of agony, but to Maxim it was a sign of life. To experience that pain, the man still had to be breathing, his heart still had to be beating, and for as long as that was happening, there would be a chance that he would be able to pull through. For him to truly have a chance, though, he would need to get to the healers as fast as possible. There was no way that they were going to be able to carry them. Their skin was too fragile and the time it would take to get them there might kill them with all of the breaks that they would need to take to change how they carried them. They needed another way to bring them to the compound and to the healers who were waiting there.

"Azra," Maxim called to the warrior helping another of the men nearby. "Do you know where Jacob is?"

"I'm here. What do you need?"

Maxim turned and saw the human man coming toward him.

"Do you know how to operate the vehicle that Jonah and Rain built?" he asked.

"I can only guess," Jacob said. "I didn't know of the technology when they were building it."

"Tell me what you know," Maxim said. "Hurry."

Maxim listened intently as Jacob told him the basic way that he thought that the vehicle was used. He nodded.

"Thank you. Is it close to here?"

"It shouldn't be too far."

"Help Azra watch over the men," he said. "Find any water that you can and pour it over their skin. Don't take their clothes or robes off of them. I'll be back as soon as I can."

Maxim stood and started running in the direction that he had seen his father coming. He pushed his feet harder and harder with each step, reaching inside of himself to find the power that his kind had given him. He rarely used the impossible speed that flowed through him, never finding the opportunity when he had truly needed it. Now, though, he knew that it was the only thing that was going to give those men the chance to live. He forced himself faster, finding the limit to his speed and breaking it, pushing his muscles beyond the boundaries that they had ever reached, until the world around him blurred with his speed and he barely felt the ground as he ran. He had to get to the vehicle that those who had come from Earth had left behind. It would bring them to the compound far faster than their feet could, not just helping them to save those men but also getting the vehicle out of the reach of the hybrid army.

AEGEUS FELT his mouth go dry and his pulse pounding in his temples. He tried to process what he had just witnessed, but he couldn't seem to wrap his mind around it. For a moment, he thought that he had been looking into the eyes of his son. The man had been standing several yards away from him and he only had the chance to see him for a brief moment, but there was something within Aegeus that told him that he had just seen Maxim, though he couldn't be sure. He tried to calm the burst of excitement that he had felt when he first saw him. He didn't want to build himself up too much only to find out that the man who he had seen was not actually his son.

But his face had been so familiar. It had seemed so right. In the young man's eyes he had seen the eyes of his first-born. Aegeus still remembered the first time that he had seen those eyes, just moments after his wife brought him into the world. He had prepared for a baby that was scream-ing, angry at the sudden change in its existence. Instead, he saw a face that was serene, disciplined in a way that usually only came with many years. Those eyes had stared up at him, reaching out to him in a still, unwavering way that connected with Aegeus instantly, and overtook everything within him. He knew in that moment that he had a son, a gift that was unlike anything that he had ever been given, anything that he had ever experienced. This child was his legacy and would be the greatest pride that he had ever felt. When Kyven was born, he loved him deeply and was proud to have another son, but Maxim was set apart. Those eyes were like his father's, as if the gaze that Aegeus had seen the moment that Maxim was born had spanned the generations and linked him to the greatest man Aegeus had ever known, a man who Maxim would never have the opportunity to meet.

It hadn't just been the young man's eyes that had reached out to Aegeus and told him that he had finally found the child that he had longed for for the years that they had been apart. The curve of his face was stronger, sharper now that it had the years of a grown man on it, but it was still the face of the little boy who had waited for him at the window until he returned home from battle and watched him with rapt attention as he told him of what he had experienced. Aegeus had always been so careful not to tell Maxim too much. There were details that he was never to know, things that happened that Aegeus had to simply pretend didn't happen at all. Instead, he would take simple moments and expand them, making them more important and more impactful than they had been so that he could make his son feel as though he had been there with him, that they weren't apart for all of those days that the battles brought him from their home. He had never wanted Maxim to go through any of the things that he had. He had hoped that the harder that he fought and the more that he put into his service to the Order, the less turmoil and conflict would exist by the time that his sons were old enough to fight. As soon as his plan for the final battle on Uoria had gone awry, though, he knew that that had been a naïve and futile aspiration. He had failed them and the rest of his kind.

Now as Aegeus watched the man run from the battle-field, he knew that he was seeing Maxim. All of the men of his kind were incredibly fast, but there had been none like his son. From the time that he was a tiny child he had run with a speed that rivaled even the men, and he knew that the older he got, the more potent that capability would be. In the few moments before he disappeared into the desert, though, Aegeus noticed that Maxim didn't look completely sure of himself. His steps seemed hesitant, as if he hadn't run in some time. This was a painful and sad thought for Aegeus. He knew that he had missed so much of his son's life. He had missed him growing tall and his face becoming so much like his own. He had missed him training for the army and serving under the King. He had missed all that he had learned and all that he had accomplished. Somehow, though, knowing that Maxim didn't run anymore like he had when he was younger cut into Aegeus more deeply. It underscored all that had changed and all that could have been had he not been captured that day on the battlefield.

The battle around Aegeus was nothing more than a loose scattering of people across what had been their battle-field and he could see the two armies splitting and heading in their own directions, leaving each other as if they had lost their determination and the drive to fight, at least for that moment. It was a strange sight, something that he knew in the back of his mind that he had witnessed countless times before, and yet he felt disoriented and out of balance watching it now. He searched his mind, trying to think back to the other battles that he had fought and how they had ended. He remembered the hardships of the battles that had resulted in horrific injuries and escaping from the fray to help those who were wounded, or to be helped himself. He remembered chasing the enemies away from the center of the clash, forcing them away until they had run, leaving only his army in place. Though he knew that there had been times that were more like this, the battle ending in both sides exiting, their energy depleted and their determination shifted to regrouping and rebuilding so that they were prepared for what they knew would be another fight on another day, it was difficult to actually recall any of those battles happening. He wished that he could now. There was so much that he wished that he could remember, that seemed to have been taken from him by the years that he had spent in Ryan's laboratory.

During his captive years Aegeus had survived by disappearing into his thoughts. He had lived within the moments that he had already had and the times that he had already spent, choosing to forget that life was continuing forward and preferring to borrow what he had already experienced to carry him through. This was far easier for him when he was first captured and Ryan held him only as himself. The scientist, so much younger then, had held him and taunted him, so pleased with himself for finally getting his hands on the powerful and aggressively hunted Aegeus. Those were the times when it was easy for Aegeus to lose himself in his own thoughts. They were still fresh and new in his mind, and he was able to access them unfettered. Whenever he pleased he could simply sink into his mind and relive the moments that he treasured the most. He would pretend that he was in Ellora's arms again. He could feel himself embracing her and the touch of her lips on his cheek. He would imagine himself playing with his sons, their laughter filling his ears and blotting out the sounds of the lab and Ryan's voice.

The longer that he was there, though, the harder it was for him to access some of the memories that he held within him. His focus narrowed and he was only able to truly experience some of the strongest and most powerful of his thoughts. This only worsened when Ryan decided that he was going to use Aegeus not just for the Mikana DNA that he offered, but for the mutated, transformed DNA that he would be able to extract if he was able to turn the man into the thing that he hated most ferociously. The transformation from being Mikana to being Klimnu was excruciating beyond anything that Aegeus would ever have expected. He fought the toxins that tried to make their way through his veins, struggling against them as if he could control the blood that beat from his heart and swept the virulent compounds through him until they were able to take over his very cells and change them. He remembered the feeling of his soul clawing for the surface, pushing through the corruption and evil that tried to take him over, fighting to keep him, at least part of him, as he had been. During his time as Klimnu, Aegeus had been blocked off from many of his thoughts and memories. He knew that the alteration affected not just his body but also his mind, amplifying the anger, viciousness, greed, and sadism that existed, if even in the tiniest of flickers, within all living creatures. If he allowed himself to reach out to those thoughts, he made them vulnerable. They could be exposed to those changes in his mind and soon he would lose the love and strength that he got from them. He would no longer be able to think of them in the beautiful way that he had, but would be bitter and angry toward them. This would allow even more of him to slip away and he feared that if enough of that happened, he would soon be beyond redemption. Aegeus was forced to surrender himself, at least partially, to the change that Ryan had caused in him. He had to give up drifting unchained through his thoughts and instead survive on only a few of his memories, reliving those days over and over again to stop him from giving up completely.

Now that Ciyrs and Elianna had brought him back, returned him to his full Mikana state, he was able to reach those memories again. He could feel himself coming back to life, restoring what he had sometimes feared was dead, and resurrecting the determination to fight against the Order and the corruption that had started there that had shifted into determination only to not let Ryan win.

Aegeus fell into step behind those who were starting across the desert, presumably toward the compound. He didn't know what would happen when they got there, but it was a step. This was the first time in so many years that he had been able to fight for what he believed, and Aegeus knew that he wasn't going to stop now. This was just beginning and there was far more to be done.

4

———

Ellora kept her eyes focused on the river beside her as she walked. They had discovered it soon after stepping through the low-overhanging branches of the tree that had encircled them when they climbed out of the tunnels and Athan had suggested that they follow it. The water would lead them through these open sections of Uoria and back to the kingdom. Stars sparkled on the surface of the dark water, shimmering through the blackness to create pricks of blue that danced and wavered as the river moved. It felt like they were so far removed from the kingdom that they would never find their way back. She had never seen this portion of the planet before or even heard something like this described. It was almost as though they had left Uoria all together and were now crossing through some unknown land. As they continued, though, Athan reassured her that this was certainly Uoria, that this was a section that he had seen before, though many years before, and that it would take time for them to get back.

The thought of walking across the planet for what might be more than a day was frightening for Ellora. They were fully exposed, completely vulnerable to the Order or to anyone else who might not wish for them to be passing this way. She wished that they were more armed, that she had brought some of the weapons from Aegeus's war room down into the tunnels with her, or that either of the men had been more prepared. Their weapons were paltry, their supplies even more so, and she worried about what that would mean for their mission. She couldn't imagine going much further without food or anything with which to make a shelter. As soon as that thought went through her mind, she felt ashamed of herself. She knew that there were countless times when her husband would leave home thinking that he was only going to be gone a short time and found himself in a far more serious and pressing situation than he expected. Those situations had put him in circumstances that were much more difficult than the ones in which she found herself now. He would have had little to eat and only the most basic of supplies. There were times when he returned home and said that he never wanted to leave the bed because of the nights that he had spent sleeping on the ground with nothing between him and the dirt but the grass and nothing over top of him but the stars.

Using these memories to strengthen her, Ellora quickened her pace, putting more energy into her feet to bring her up so that she walked alongside Athan.

"Will we arrive back to the kingdom tonight?" she asked.

Athan shook his head, not turning to look at her.

"No," he said. "It will likely be tomorrow afternoon, maybe even tomorrow evening before we get there."

Ellora shook her head, not knowing what to make out of his answer.

"I don't understand," she said. "We didn't go that far in the tunnels. We didn't run through them for an entire day.

How could we possibly be that far away from the kingdom now?"

She noticed Athan glance back over his shoulder at Mhavrych, who had been walking along behind them since they had climbed out of the tunnels.

"There are things about the Order that no one understands," Mhavrych answered. "That includes their surroundings and the things that they have within them as much as the people."

"That doesn't make sense," Ellora argued. "We could only be as far away from the kingdom as we traveled inside of the tunnels."

"And yet we aren't."

She didn't like the answer or the way that it made her feel, but she knew that there was no point in arguing any further. They weren't going to tell her anything. Aegeus had been clear with her about the secretiveness of the Order. He told her far more than he was permitted to tell, and even that had been only the most basic of details. She had the feeling that there was much about it that even those within its most sacred of circles didn't know and didn't understand, and even if they did, they weren't going to share it with her. She would just have to trust that they were going to do what was best and ensure that she could do for her husband what she should have done so long before.

"How much longer are we going to go tonight?" she asked after several long moments of silence.

"Until our legs can't carry us any further," Athan said. "As soon as we stop, we are in more danger. The faster that we can get back to the kingdom and find Creia, the better chances we have to survive this and get to Penthos."

~

THE SUN WAS hot overhead by the time that they could see the kingdom ahead of them the next day. Ellora felt a wave of relief as she saw the stone wall that surrounded the kingdom, feeling as though they were finally nearing home and the protection that awaited there, but she could see the two men tensing.

"The Order is going to be looking for us," Athan said. "By now they would have scoured the tunnels. They know that we got out. They will have people scattered across the planet searching for us, and even more around the border of the kingdom looking for any sign of our return. Getting inside and to Creia is going to be the most dangerous part of this journey. If they capture us, we'll wish that we died getting out of the tunnels."

Ellora's mind was swimming and her body felt weak. They had found some berries and a few nuts when they were walking, but she was still hungry and the lack of adequate food was making it difficult to concentrate. She knew what Athan had said was extremely important, but she couldn't process it, almost as though her mind wouldn't allow her to.

"What are we going to do?" she finally asked.

"Mhavrych," Athan said. "How did you get back here from Penthos? Did you ride in the ship with the others?"

"No," the other man said. "I have my own ways of traveling."

"What are they?" Athan asked. Mhavrych looked hesitant, as if reluctant to share with them how he was able to move from planet to planet quickly and without the benefit of a ship to bring him. "You need to tell us," Athan said, recognizing the hesitation.

"I can't," Mhavrych said. "I've been sworn."

Ellora saw Athan take a threatening step toward the man.

"I don't know who you are or what you are doing here, but I do know that you need to start cooperating with us. The only reason that I trust you at all is that you say that you knew Aegeus."

"I do know Aegeus," Mhavrych said forcefully. "I have known him since before he left Uoria."

"Yet you won't tell us how."

"I can't," he repeated. "There are things that can't be said. I've been sworn to protect them."

"Loyalties no longer apply, Mhavrych," Athan said. "We have betrayed the Order and the oaths that we once made. All that matters now is survival. If you know a way that we can get into that kingdom and find Creia without the Order finding us, you have to tell us. Whatever it is that you are protecting is not going to be any good if we don't even make it across this field alive. Even if most of them don't know who you are or what you are doing here, you aren't safe. They were going to kill Ellora without a second thought. Don't think that they would hesitate to do the same to you."

Mhavrych stared back at Athan. The look in his eyes was fierce, almost threatening. Ellora could see in them that this man was not afraid, not even of the threat of death. Whatever it was that he was defending was far more important to him than his own life and he would be ready and willing to lay down his life in order to ensure that it was guarded properly. His eyes flickered over to Ellora and she saw something more in them. There was a pull, a lingering draw of emotion that seemed to be inspired by looking at her.

"For Aegeus," Mhavrych said. "Only for Aegeus. He trusted me and I will do what I can for him."

"Thank you," Ellora said.

"Come with me," Mhavrych told them without acknowledging her.

There was no fondness for her in his agreement to help them get inside the kingdom. He only cared about protecting what he had taken out of the tunnel and honoring Aegeus.

Ellora and Athan fell into step behind Mhavrych as he moved quickly away from where they had been standing. Rather than moving toward the kingdom, he seemed to be walking along in front of it, heading past it as quickly as he could go. When they were beyond it, he turned sharply and headed away from it, his back toward the stone wall that had been the only promise of hope for Ellora.

"Where are we going?" she asked.

Mhavrych ignored her and continued forward, leaving her with no other option but to follow along with him or turn back, attempting to enter the kingdom on her own and without even the modicum of protection that was offered by having the men with her. She glanced up at Athan and knew that there really wasn't a choice. Without the men, she was far more vulnerable. She didn't understand the Order the way that they did, she didn't know what they were going to do or what they were capable of should they find her, especially on her own. She had to go along with Mhavrych, even if she didn't know where they were going or what he might expect them to do. She had to believe that if this man knew her husband and had gained his trust, she could trust him as well.

They continued on for what felt like hours, stopping only to drink water from a small creek that they found and to eat from a grove of trees. Finally Mhavrych led them through a thicket of trees to a larger part of the same creek. The trees around them were so thick that they blocked out the evening sun until it was nearly dark. He walked out onto a large boulder and turned to face them.

"Come here," he said.

They walked out onto the rock with him, Ellora stepping up as close to Athan as she could out of fear of falling into the water beneath. When they were standing close to him, Mhavrych looked at both for a few seconds. Without saying anything or giving any warning, he reached down and grabbed onto their wrists. Ellora gasped as she felt Mhavrych drag them both forward and jumped into the water. His grip was firm and tight, preventing her from fighting away from him beneath the cold water.

Ellora expected the water to be shallow at this portion of the creek and was shocked when she felt them continuing to sink. She thrashed against his grip again, but he only held her more tightly, forcing her closer to his side as he kicked through the water so that they moved backwards. Ellora tried to see the surface, but they had gone so far beneath the water that she couldn't even see the slight amount of light that had been available to them before they went below the water. Her lungs were starting to burn with the small amount of breath that she was able to catch in them before they broke through the surface and she worried that she was not going to be able to survive long enough to break free of Mhavrych's grasp and get out of the water. She could feel herself slipping away and was nearly giving up when she felt her head emerge from the water.

Though it was still dark around her, she could feel the air touching her skin and she dragged it into her lungs eagerly. She could hear Athan gasping for breath the way that she was and knew that he hadn't expected the dive off of the boulder into the creek, either. Mhavrych was still gripping their wrists and she felt his fingers tighten down into her skin even harder as he pulled her arm up out of the water. An instant later she felt her hand touch a slick, cold rock surface and her fingertips graze across small sections that felt rougher than the rest.

"What..." she started to protest, but before she could get the rest of the words out, she felt like she was being dragged forward toward the stones.

Ellora tried to resist the pull as she had with Mhavrych's grip, but there was nothing that she could do. She noticed that it wasn't Mhavrych that was pulling her, but something else, like an unseen force that was dragging her away from where they were still partly submerged in the water. In what could have been several minutes or just a matter of seconds, she felt the water around her disappear and pressure close in around her. Ellora didn't know what was happening and she fought to swallow down the fear that was filling her. Finally her body hit something solid. Disoriented, she didn't know if she had come into contact with the same stone that she had been touching or if she had fallen back through the water and was now on the bottom of the creek. She couldn't feel any water near her though and after a few moments she realized that she was breathing comfortably and easily.

"We need to keep going," Mhavrych said from beside her.

Ellora noticed that he wasn't holding onto her any longer and she opened her eyes. It seemed far later in the night now and she became aware of a biting cold as she looked around and saw that they were now standing in what looked like an open field. The grass wasn't tall and waving, but rather scrubby and a pale color that seemed to glow in the moonlight. Athan was still pulling himself off of the ground and Mhavrych reached down to take him by his elbow and drag him up to his feet.

"How much further to the kingdom?" Ellora asked.

Mhavrych looked at her and gave a short, almost mocking laugh.

"Much farther than you could understand," he said.

He started walking, not looking back as if he simply expected that the other two would follow him. They continued along, the terrain becoming less and less familiar as they walked. Massive rocks seemed to grow up out of the grass and then dipped down into sand that led to another deep pool of water. Ellora braced herself to jump into the water again, but Mhavrych led them around the edge and to a row of scraggly trees at the edge of the water. When they reached one of them, he crouched down and brushed sand away from the base. In one fast movement he grabbed onto their wrists again and pulled their hands forward to touch the damp bark. She expected to feel only the cold softness of the tree, but instead she felt something hard, like a stone embedded in it. Before she could ask what was happening, she felt the same pulling, dragging feeling that she had felt when they were in the water, and then the pressure closing in around her.

Ellora tried to relax into the feeling this time. She knew that there was nothing else that she could do. She couldn't fight the pulling feeling and there was nothing that she could do to stop whatever was happening to her. The feeling lasted longer this time and blackness started to press down on her. She didn't want to let it take over. She wanted to stay in control, but soon she couldn't resist it any longer.

She didn't know how long she had been lying in the grass when awareness finally returned to her. She could feel someone's hand patting her cheek, trying to rouse her, and she willed her eyes to open. Athan's face was close to hers when her eyes opened and she felt relieved to see him. To one side she could see Mhavrych pacing, his steps tight and small as his eyes scanned their surroundings.

"Can you get up?" Athan asked.

"How long have I been here?" Ellora asked.

"A few minutes."

"We need to go," Mhavrych said, his voice sounding tighter and more anxious than it had before.

She didn't like him compelling them forward again. She didn't want to go through that feeling again and feel like she was getting further and further from what she knew. At this point, though, there was nothing else that she could do but what he said. She didn't know where they were or how far they had gone, and would have no means of survival if she was alone.

Athan helped her to her feet and Ellora looked around. Everything looked familiar and she felt a sense of calm come over her as she realized that they were in the orchard of the kingdom, just within the barrier of the stone wall. While they were still a distance from the village, this was an area of the kingdom that was rarely used by anyone, particularly now that Idella was gone and it was only Lila who had any use for the home there. Most of the rest who lived in the kingdom either went to the far side of the orchard to gather food or waited until it was gathered by others and purchased or traded for it. This meant that it was far less likely that the Order would have people patrolling this area in as thick a concentration as they would in other areas, giving them much more opportunity to slip through the kingdom and into the village undetected.

"How did we do that?" Athan asked as they started forward through the orchard. "I didn't recognize either of those places."

"We did it because we had to," Mhavrych answered. "There was no other way."

"I don't understand," Ellora said. "We barely went anywhere, how could we possibly have traveled as far as we just did? Where were we?"

Mhavrych stopped and turned to look at Ellora sharply. There was an intensity on his face that told Ellora that he was done listening to her questions and wasn't going to go any further in his explanation of how they just traveled than he thought he needed to. She nearly took a step back from him, but held her ground.

"We traveled in the way that we had to travel," Mhavrych told her. "It is the way that I get around when I have to, and the way that I got from Penthos back here to Uoria without detection. That's what was asked of me, wasn't it?"

"But don't you think that if we traveled that way, we should know how we did it? That we should know where we've been?" Athan asked.

"Would it be of any consequence to you if you did know?" Mhavrych asked, turning his attention to Athan. "Would it, in any way, change where we are now or what we have left ahead of us to accomplish?" Athan stared at him blankly, visibly unable to come up with an answer that he thought was appropriate. Mhavrych gave a slight nod. "Exactly. There are things that you do not need to understand to follow. Every day you do things because you think or know that you should do them without ever asking why. As a member of the Order, that applies more to you than to anyone else. This is one of those things. Either you continue to trust me and come with me the rest of the way to the village, or you are on your own. If you choose to be on your own, that is final. I will not protect you or help you in any way. You will be as the rest of the Order are to me. If you come along with me, you are to tell no one about how we traveled back to the kingdom. Nothing. Until I have decided who can be trusted to know anything that has happened, you are not to speak of it to anyone. Do you understand?"

Ellora wanted to resist. It was her instinct to push back against the aggression in the man's voice and demand to know more about what was happening, but just as it had in the tunnels, Aegeus's voice came to her, calming her. It told her to remain faithful to the promise that she had made him, to fulfill what he had started and protect the planet and their kind with everything that was in her. In her mind her husband soothed her and told her to be still in her strength and her determination, and trust Mhavrych as she would trust him. All would be made clear if she could only reach within herself and find the drive and the faith that he had within him when he walked into battle. She reminded herself that it was Mhavrych that had rescued her from the tunnel, even though he didn't have to. He could have allowed her to run through them until she tired and collapsed, or until she found her way back into the snare of the Order members who were pursuing her so violently. It would have been a distraction that could have benefitted him, making it easier for him to get out of the tunnels rather than having to help her and then Athan. Yet he didn't. He offered his help to her without question, and it was up to her to offer her trust to him in the same way.

5

—————

Athan could nearly feel the eyes of the Order on them as they made their way through the orchard. It was so quiet in this section of the kingdom, as if it had been preserved as the last moment that Idella knew it and when she died the energy had been taken from it as well. Even in the stillness, though, he felt as though they were being pursued, always just steps from one of the members of the Order coming at them and taking them prisoner. His hand tightened around the handle of his sword at that thought. He had already witnessed his dearest friend taken prisoner and though he had yet to see him since discovering that he was still alive, Athan knew that Aegeus had gone through pure torture for the years that they had been apart. He had sacrificed himself, giving of his very life, to counteract the corruption of the Order and bring down the forces that were threatening Uoria and all of the Universe. He owed it to Aegeus and all of those years to stand strong against the enemy and swear to not be taken.

He walked close beside Ellora as they followed Mhavrych. His mind was still churning as he looked at the younger man's back. He couldn't understand who this man was or what he could have meant to Aegeus. He seemed so young and his face wasn't at all familiar. It didn't hold even the hint of features that Athan knew from his past and he knew that Aegeus had never mentioned his name to him before. Mhavrych had confirmed that Athan wouldn't have known about him, and that Aegeus wouldn't have told him about him, but that only made the situation seem more confusing. Aegeus and he had been inseparable for most of their lives. Though he was older than Aegeus, he had always respected him and the closeness of their bond had been unlike any other friendship that he had ever experienced. He had always shared everything with Aegeus and thought that his best friend had done the same for him. Not telling him about Mhavrych meant either that their friendship was not as close as Athan believed it to be, or that whatever Mhavrych meant to the mission that Aegeus had made for himself was so serious that he couldn't even reach out to his most trusted of companions for help.

The crack of a branch in the near distance stopped Athan's thoughts and stiffened his spine. He instinctively reached for Ellora and brought her closer to him, sweeping her to his side rather than in front or behind him because he couldn't decipher from which direction the sound had come. Mhavrych had obviously heard the sound as well and was paused in his place, his hand hovering over the blade in his waistband. Athan saw his eyes flickering around the trees, trying to see through the thickening darkness to what created the sound. The men's eyes met and Mhavrych gave a slight nod backwards.

"We need to keep moving," he said, his voice lower. "We aren't far from the edge of the orchard. Once we get there, we need to avoid the buildings that don't usually have people in them and stay to the main road."

"Won't they expect us there?" Ellora asked.

Athan shook his head.

"No," he said. "The Order thinks logically, but sometimes that means overlooking what might really happen. To them, the logical thing would be for us to go to the smaller side roads to avoid the main road because we would think that they would be on the main road, so they will go to the side roads. There might still be someone patrolling the main road, but we will have a better chance there. Move quickly, and as soon as you see anyone you recognize as not being a part of the Order, get their attention. Be as loud as you can. It doesn't matter what you say or what you talk about when you get near them, just bring as much focus to you as you possibly can."

"Why would we do that?" Ellora asked. "Don't we want to get to the village and find Creia without anyone noticing?"

"The Order doesn't want to be detected. There is nothing strange about you walking through the kingdom. You live here. You always have. And you have known Athan for many years. No one would question the two of you being together. The Order, though, does not want to seem out of place. They wouldn't want to risk anyone seeing one of their members confront you and then have you disappear. The more attention that you bring to yourselves, the less likely it is for someone in the Order to come out and try to take you prisoner."

"Why are you talking as though it is only the two of us who are continuing on?" Athan asked. "Aren't you coming with us?"

"I'll go with you for as far as I can," Mhavrych said. "I

cannot guarantee that I will be able to be with you the whole way."

"What would stop you?" Athan asked.

Mhavrych shook his head.

"I'll go with you as far as I can."

They started out of the orchard again and Athan took a final glance back over his shoulder. As he did, he thought he noticed movement behind a nearby tree and the hint of a face disappear from view.

Mhavrych's warning reverberated through his mind as they continued toward the village. He didn't understand what would stop the man from being with them the entire way, especially considering it had been him who had been so insistent that they get away from the planet as quickly as possible. Now that Athan knew that he traveled far distances without needing a ship, however, he realized that there was very little that he really needed from the two of them. Him going along with them was for another purpose, though he didn't quite know what that purpose could be.

Just as they had planned, they got to the edge of the orchard and increased their pace. They made it to the main road that led through the kingdom and into the main village. He looked around at the buildings in this section of the kingdom that were rarely used. There were emergency shelters and supply houses, extra homes for visiting species and even the occasional abandoned house or shop from generations past. They steered clear of these buildings, knowing that they were the least likely to have anyone near them, and therefore the most likely to have members of the Order hiding within or around them, ready to swoop down on the insurgents.

The feeling of their eyes on him was getting stronger. He knew that he was imagining it, but he felt as though they were all around him, scrutinizing his every movement, their judging gaze burning into him as they shot hatred of him and his betrayal through his body. Mhavrych remained in his place in front of him, and Athan found himself hoping that he didn't leave. He didn't know why. It might have been the growing sense of camaraderie and kinship that was building among them as they traveled across the planet. It might have been a simple sense of uncertainty about the man that made him uncomfortable with the idea of him disappearing and him not knowing where he went or what he might be doing. Whatever the reason, Athan wanted to keep his eyes on Mhavrych and ensure that they remained near one another, at least until they returned to the village and were somewhat safer.

They pushed themselves faster, running now as they made their way along the main road toward the more populated area of the kingdom. The sense that they were being watched was only increasing with every step and out of the corner of his eye Athan saw a figure step out from around the corner of a small building used during the harvest to store food before it was processed and distributed. He touched his hand to Ellora's back and applied pressure, pushing her to move faster. He wanted to call out to Mhavrych, but his voice wouldn't come. He didn't want the Order member to know that he had seen him. Somehow that seemed that it would put them in even greater danger.

Behind them the man had walked out onto the main road and was following them, keeping his pace steady so that he was approaching them rapidly. Athan felt panic start to form in his belly. It was only one man, but that meant that there were others. He remembered the early training that he had gone through when he was first initiated into the organization. They were taught to always remain in close enough proximity to one another that even if it looked as though they were alone, several others could be at their side in a matter of moments to ensure that they were protected and that they were able to complete the mission that they had be sent to fulfill.

They continued to run and Athan saw another figure join the first. This one held a weapon in his hand and Athan knew that at any instant the figure could throw it, grievously wounding whoever it hit. He pushed Ellora slightly harder and they caught up to Mhavrych so that soon the three were running beside one another, creating a line across the road. It made Athan feel as though they were more vulnerable, but at the same time, it meant that none were in front and none were behind. They were all equal.

It was obvious that the other two could hear the footsteps of the Order members coming toward them now, but neither relented to look back over their shoulders. Ahead of them Athan saw another figure step out into the road and his heart leapt into his throat. They were surrounded now. with two men behind and at least one in front, they had little chance of overcoming the Order. As they continued forward, no other option to fuel them in another direction, however, Athan realized that the figure ahead of them was not a member of the Order sent to find them. Relief swept through him as the young, familiar face came into full view. Gathering all of the strength within him and fighting through the fear that told him to stay quiet, he shouted.

"Kyven!"

The name burst out of him and he saw the figure pause, turning in their direction. Ellora let out a sound much like a sob beside him and then Athan heard her scream out her son's name as well. Athan repeated it, yelling louder this time as they continued down the road.

"Mama?" Kyven called. "Athan? What are you doing here?"

Athan could hear the sound of the footsteps behind them lessening and when he looked back he noticed the last bit of a tunic disappearing around the corner of one of the buildings. The Order members were no longer pursuing them. For now, they were safe.

A smile came to Athan's lips as he watched Ellora gather her younger son into her arms for a warm, affectionate embrace.

"How are you?" she asked, leaning back to look into Kyven's face. "Are you alright?" She took her hands from around his back and settled them on either side of his face. "Have you healed?"

Kyven looked at his mother with an expression of affection, but also that Ellora was worrying heedlessly. He nodded.

"I'm fine," he said. "Well, I'm almost fine. I'm nearly healed. I don't think that there is much more than can be done other than just letting my body get better on its own. The healings and the treatments have done all that they can."

Athan could see Ellora's shoulders lower with relief.

"Good," she said. Her smile faded and she looked around as if just noticing where they were. "What are you doing out here?"

Kyven stepped back to allow his mother's hands to fall away from his face.

"I've been laying around trying to get better for too long. I needed to do something. There are so many extra people in the kingdom right now that they are running out of food. I volunteered to come out here and get some of the food stores. What are you and Athan doing here?"

Ellora began to stammer some sort of response, but Kyven didn't seem to notice. His eyes had fallen on Mhavrych and his expression had shifted. It was tense now, a look of surprise on it that wasn't necessarily pleased. Ellora noticed that he was looking at the other man and stopped talking. She looked back and forth between them, then began to speak.

"We really shouldn't keep everybody waiting," Athan said loudly, grasping hold of Ellora's elbow with one hand and the back of Kyven's shoulder with the other. "There are a lot of people who are going to be hungry if we don't get some food to them soon."

He needed to keep them moving. They couldn't stop here and Athan knew that the thoughts churning through Kyven's mind were too much for him to confront right then. They needed to gather the food that Kyven had come to retrieve and get back to the village so that they could talk to Creia.

Athan stepped up to the nearest food storage building and opened the door cautiously. He looked inside before stepping out of the way and allowing Kyven to enter. Together they gathered armfuls of bags and crates and carried them out. Mhavrych followed behind them and took up two large barrels that he tucked one beneath each arm. Ellora scooped up a bag and then closed the door. They started toward the village at a slower pace than they had approached, but still faster than they usually would. The look on Kyven's face told him that he knew something more was happening than they had told him, but Athan wasn't going to share anything with him while they still might be near the seeking ears of the Order.

Finally they reached the edge of the village. He felt calmer and more relaxed as they made their way through the homes and shops, then on toward the meeting hall. Though he knew that they were far from completely out of danger, now that they were in a more crowded place they were more secure than they had been when out in the open crossing the planet and making their way through the back of the kingdom. Mhavrych was still with them, which was reassuring to Athan, but he still wasn't completely at ease. They walked into the meeting hall and dropped off the food that they had brought, which was immediately scooped up by the women who were preparing meals for the visitors.

"Have you seen Creia?" Athan asked Kyven.

Kyven nodded.

"He's in the back with Rey. What's going on? You still haven't told me what you were doing in the back of the kingdom, and I didn't see you for the last two days. What's happening?"

"We need to talk to Creia. It's urgent. We'll explain everything when we can, but for now we just need to talk to him."

They made their way through the meeting hall and to the massive stone door that blocked Rey's private chamber from the rest of the hall. Athan used the large carved knocker to announce their presence and almost immediately the door opened. Creia's eyes widened when he saw them.

"Sir, can we speak with you?" Athan asked.

Creia nodded.

"Absolutely." He stepped out of the way to allow the small group to enter the chamber with him and then closed the door. "Has something happened?"

"We have reason to believe that the Order is more corrupt than we originally thought," Athan said. "Ellora went down into their lair and they threatened her. The three of us nearly didn't escape with our lives. It has taken us two days to return here because we have been trying to avoid them."

"Why are they threatening Ellora?" Creia asked.

Athan and Ellora exchanged glances. They hadn't told him about Aegeus and Athan was still hesitant to do so. Though Ryan had confirmed to those in the ship that Aegeus had not been killed in the battle as had been the belief of everyone in the kingdom for so many years, he also suggested that he might not be alive for long. There was always the chance that the scientist had already eliminated Aegeus now that he had found his sons, and Athan didn't want to tell Creia that he was still alive only to find that he had actually been killed just days before. At the same time, however, it was critical that the Denynso king understand the severity of the situation and the gravity of the threat that the Order posed to Ellora and to the rest of them so that he would be willing to act as promptly and effectively as possible. Ellora gave a small nod and Athan turned back to Creia. He took a step toward him and saw Rey stand from the chair where he had been sitting.

"Aegeus didn't die in the battle," Athan said, trying to choose his words carefully. "When we were on Penthos, Ryan told us that he was still alive."

"Alive?" Rey asked, coming toward them, his eyes wide. "What do you mean he's alive? Where has he been?"

Athan took a breath. He needed them to stay calm. They couldn't afford any hysteria that might bring too much attention to them. He noticed that Mhavrych was sinking back away from the two leaders, trying to stay out of sight. Athan was still confused by his actions, not understanding what was causing him to be so evasive even while trying to help them. For now he couldn't concentrate on that. He needed to inform the Kings of what was happening so that they could make the decisions that needed to be made.

Aware of Ellora's presence and the impact that what he was going to say would make on her, Athan told Rey and Creia what they had learned when they were on Penthos. He explained the Valdicians appearing on the ship and the image of Ryan that had told them of the danger that was awaiting them. He could see their faces darkening, the anger building even more as he gave more details than he had before, but he continued forward, pushing forward to describe Ellora going down to confront the Order and the threat that they now posed. The confusion radiating off of Rey was palpable and Athan felt guilt gnawing at his belly.

"The Order?" Rey asked.

Creia looked at Athan darkly. He knew that he should have called Creia out of the room to discuss this. Rey didn't know about the Order or what they did, and telling him could have put the entire kingdom, and everything that they had already done, at risk. Athan took another step toward the King, looking at him imploringly.

"I'm sorry, Rey," he said.

"I am King," Rey said. "I should know everything that is happening within my kingdom."

"It isn't just you," Athan tried to explain. "The majority of the kingdom doesn't know about the Order."

"That's unacceptable," Rey said, his usually calm and gentle demeanor breaking under the obvious distress that he was feeling. "As King of the Mikana it is my responsibility to take care of my people and make sure that they are properly protected and managed. How am I –"

"Sometimes taking care of your people means accepting that you don't know everything," Mhavrych said, cutting Rey off as he stepped forward, finally revealing his presence fully to the Kings. "You are no different than the kings of the Mikana that came before you. In the earliest days of the Order, the King was a part of it, but that changed. For many generations now, the rule of the kingdom and the control of the Order have been separate. It is better that way. You have been kept from knowing about the Order and its responsibilities for a reason, and that reason has not changed. The fact that you know of it now makes no difference. You are not a part of the Order. You have no say in its operations and no control over it. You will not be able to resolve its corruption on your own, and when we have found victory over those who have corrupted it, it will carry on as it has... without your interference. Do you understand?"

Rey looked taken aback by Mhavrych's boldness and his mouth opened and closed a few times before he spoke.

"Who are you to tell me what I am allowed to know or what I am permitted to do within my kingdom?" he asked angrily. "It is clear that you are not even Mikana. You are not a member of my kingdom. What authority do you have over me or over any of my kind?"

Mhavrych drew close to Rey, his jaw set and no intimidation on his face or in his stance. There was a long, still pause and Athan could feel the tension building in the room. Finally Mhavrych spoke.

"You will never know who I am or why I matter. It is not for you to know. You are not the Order. You will never be the Order. What I am means more to you and to all of the Universe than you could ever understand. The sooner that you accept that, the better the chances will be that all of you will survive."

Athan stepped up to Mhavrych's side and looked at the Kings.

"It is urgent that we get off of Uoria as soon as possible.

The Order is now turned against Ellora, Mhavrych, and me. They will turn against any who is aligned with us and everyone will be vulnerable. Because of the nature of the Order, they are a hidden threat, a disguised danger. I have only recently learned that even I do not know all of the men who are members. That means that we have no way of knowing who in this kingdom we can really trust."

"What are we to do?" Creia asked.

"We need to get to Penthos," Ellora said. "My husband and my other son are waiting there. There is a war happening and the only hope that any of us have is to fight in it. Getting us off of Uoria will protect us from the Order here, but it will also mean giving them the help that they need on the battlefield. We have to defeat Ryan and the army that he created."

"I don't understand what any of this has to do with each other," Rey said. "You said that the Order has been around for many generations. Even if generations before Ryan started the experiments that he is doing now, they could not have started this, they couldn't be the beginning of the Order."

"There are still many things that we need to figure out," Athan admitted. "We are just now unraveling what all of this means. What matters now is that we get off of Uoria and to Penthos. From there we will be able to bring this all to a close."

"We will leave tomorrow," Creia said. "We'll gather everyone into the ship and be to Penthos as soon as possible."

Athan started to agree, but saw Kyven shaking his head out of the corner of his eye.

"We can't do that," Kyven said.

"Why?" Creia asked. "The danger is only going to

continue to build. Athan already said that we won't be able to recognize the members of the Order and that means that the longer we stay here, the more danger that we are all in. They could come for us at any time and we would never be able to get to Penthos to help Maxim and those who are there."

Kyven shook his head again.

"Leaving now could be just as dangerous. I have seen Penthos and the army that they are facing there. No matter how dedicated the people here who want to go with us are, they are not prepared for what they will experience. They need all of the preparation possible. We need as much food and water as we can gather and get onto the ship, and the army needs to be trained. Besides, Rain hasn't returned from the settlement. We need her to pilot the ship and the people she has with her to boost our numbers. We have to stay here, at least for a time. We need to be ready if we are going to give any benefit to those who are waiting for us on Penthos. An untrained, unprepared army will be more dangerous than no army at all."

"How will Athan and Ellora remain safe?" Rey asked. "We don't know the faces of the Order. They could come in to our homes, into our training grounds, and destroy us without anyone ever realizing it."

"No," Ellora said, her voice sounding as though a realization was just settling into her mind. "No, they won't try that. Remember what Athan said. They don't want to call attention to themselves, especially now that Mhavrych is with us."

"What does he have to do with protecting us?" Rey asked.

"Aegeus knew Mhavrych, but even Athan didn't know him. He is someone far more important than any of us understand right now and his existence has been hidden away for so long. They might want to destroy him, but they also know that his very presence among us means that we are aware of the threat. As long as we stay vigilant, we can do everything possible to stay safe. We accept only those we know into our training grounds. No one is ever alone. We speak to no one about what is really happening. Those who are willing to fight must be willing to do so without having all of the information. If they press for more, they are removed. That is the way that it is going to have to be. Rain and her kind will be here soon. We should be ready to leave in no more than a week."

"Will those on Penthos be able to hold the hybrid army off until then?" Creia asked.

"All we can do is have faith in them," Kyven said. "And know that they will stay strong until we are able to be there to end this before it can get any worse."

6

———

Jonah dropped the final match to the bathroom counter just as he heard the front door close on the floor below. He hurried out of the bathroom and rushed down the stairs to greet Aubrey. As she had every other day that she had returned home from work that week she looked exhausted and completely depleted of every bit of energy and spirit that had been within her. The large bag that she usually carried across her chest and hanging by her hip fell from her hand and slumped to the floor. She lifted her eyes to him as she shrugged out of her jacket and Jonah saw a slight smile come to her lips. That was a moment that he looked forward to every day. Though he hated that she was so exhausted and everything that she had to go through each day, it always made his heart soar when she returned home in the evening and looked so happy that he was there waiting for her.

"Another hard day?" he asked, coming down the steps and reaching for her jacket.

Aubrey nodded.

"I honestly think this project is going to be the death of

me. They wanted me to stay even later, but I couldn't do it. I told them that I was going to grab a bite to eat and I escaped."

"Aren't they going to notice that you're gone?" Jonah asked with a laugh.

"I don't know," Aubrey said. "At some point they'll probably realize that they've been talking to my empty chair for a while. I don't care, though. I just couldn't be in that lab for another minute. My brain seriously might have just liquefied. They might be mad when I get back there tomorrow, but I'll come up with some sort of excuse as to what happened to me."

"Like what?" Jonah asked, carrying the jacket down the short hallway leading off of the entryway so that he could hang it in the closet.

"I'm not sure. Maybe I was horribly allergic to whatever I ate for supper and I ended up in the hospital."

"They wouldn't ask for a doctor's note or anything?"

Aubrey let out a long sigh.

"They probably would. Alright. Well then maybe I had a car accident."

"Again. Doctor's note."

"I just can't catch a break."

Jonah laughed again and held his arms open to her. Aubrey stepped into them and sighed as she nuzzled her face into his chest. This wasn't the same sigh as she had just released. That was exasperation and exhaustion, frustration and resignation. This was happiness and contentment, a sense of safety and comfort that came from being cradled in his arms. He loved that sound and the feeling that it gave him each time that he heard it.

"Well," he said, taking her by the shoulders and gently guiding her down the hallway back toward the stairs, "what if I keep brainstorming that excuse note for you while you relax. I have a surprise for you."

"You do?" Aubrey asked as they made their way up the stairs toward their bedroom. "I could really use something wonderful right now."

"I can't promise wonderful," Jonah said, guiding her into the bathroom, "but I hope that you like it."

Aubrey gasped as she saw the candles strewn across the counter and along the edge of the bathtub. Plush white bubbles floated invitingly on the surface of the water, the dancing light from the candles causing them to shimmer.

"This is incredible," she said, turning toward Jonah with a look of pure joy on her face. "Thank you so much."

"Of course," Jonah said. "I know how hard you've been working and I wanted to do something to help you relax. I am so proud of everything that you do and I wanted you to know that I'm here to support and encourage you in any way that I can. Even if that is just drawing a bubble bath for you so that you can relax at the end of the day."

Aubrey rose up on her toes to touch a kiss to his lips then stepped back to kick off her shoes then start undressing. Jonah watched as she peeled away each layer of clothing, revealing the luscious body that he craved every moment. When she was completely naked, she reached back and swept her hair up off of her neck. Jonah's mouth began to water as she wound her thick mane around, causing her breasts to rise and press toward him. She secured her hair with a clip and then stepped down into the water.

The bubbles rose up around her as Aubrey settled down into the water, coming over her breasts and concealing her body. Even as the bubbles covered her, Jonah felt himself desiring her more. It was as though the idea of removing the bubbles, revealing her to him again, was sending his arousal spiraling up. Aubrey rested her head on the wall and reclined back with her eyes closed for a few seconds before turning toward him. Her eyes opened slowly and she gave a small smile.

"There sure is a lot of room in this tub," she said. "I could use some company."

Jonah grinned and undressed, adding his clothes to the pile of hers on the floor. She sat up so that he could take his place behind her, settling down into the water with his legs on either side of her. Aubrey sat back so that she rested on his chest and stomach and her head tucked against his neck. Jonah brought his hands down over her shoulders and ran them down so that they traced the swell of her breasts. He could feel the taut peaks of her nipples against his palms were already tight and hardening in response to his touch. His body was doing the same and he lifted his hips to press into her back, hoping to silently express his desire to her. She responded by running her hands down his thighs and stroking her body back against him. Jonah ducked his head and kissed along the side of her neck.

When he had first decided to draw the bath for her, he had intended it as a way for her to spend some time to herself away from all of the pressures of her day at work, but now that he was in the water with her, he knew that this was so much better. He wanted to hold her, to comfort her and show her that she was the most precious thing in his life. The work that they were doing was still incredibly important to him, but there were times when he felt as though it were getting in between the two of them. Though their connection was still as strong as it had always been, he felt like they didn't have as much time as he would want to just enjoy being together. There were always reminders of the strange way that they came together, and the efforts that filled nearly every moment that they had. From the moment that Aubrey got home until they both fell asleep, they researched and brainstormed. He spent the time that she was at work coming up with further ideas to research and going back over everything that they had already figured out. Locking themselves away in the bathtub together felt like they were stealing these moments for themselves, closing themselves off, if only for a short time, from everything else so that they could concentrate just on each other.

Jonah let his hands run across her breasts again and then down onto her belly. It shivered beneath his touch and he tightened his thighs around her. Aubrey's back arched slightly as his fingers ran along the plane of her belly and into the dip between her hipbones. He traced the valley, letting his fingers move onto each bone as he tenderly teased her skin. Aubrey whimpered and lifted her body up so that it rose subtly on his. She pressed her thighs apart, inviting him to touch her, and Jonah didn't resist.

His wife's body was warm and wet waiting for his fingers and she moaned with pleasure as he glided them down into her delicate folds. He continued to kiss along her neck as he touched her, exploring her indulgently and reverently. Her mouth opened and she gasped, furthering his need for her and encouraging Jonah to enter her. His fingers slid easily within her and he felt the luscious warmth of her walls embracing them. Jonah turned his hand just enough to press the pad of his thumb to her peak. He applied gentle pressure and swirled his touch in a small circle. Aubrey's fingers dug into the muscles of his thighs and out of the corner of his eye he could see her biting down onto her bottom lip.

Jonah wrapped his other hand around her ribcage and

cupped it over her breast so that he could knead into her soft, pliant flesh as he continued to let his fingers press into her. His fingers glided in and out of her, giving him new perspective of the ridges and dips of the inside of her body. He imagined the feeling on his cock and felt himself harden even further.

Suddenly Aubrey gasped and sat up straighter. He hadn't felt her climax, but she was pulling away from him, folding her legs under her body to stand up.

"What's wrong?" he asked.

"Nothing's wrong," Aubrey said as she climbed out of the tub and grabbed one of the towels that were sitting on the shelf on the wall. "I think I might have just figured something out."

She swept the towel around her body, tucking the end in between the breasts that he had been stroking and wished were still in his hands. Jonah watched her as she rushed out of the bathroom, a feeling of disappointment sinking into his belly. Finally he climbed up out of the tub and followed her out of the bathroom, taking a towel as he went. Aubrey was sitting on the window seat when he stepped into the bedroom. Still in her towel, she looked just as desirable as she had in the tub, but the look on her face no longer seemed interested in him. Instead, she was focused intently on the book in her lap and the notebook that she had spread open on a small table beside her.

"What are you doing?" he asked.

Aubrey looked up at him.

"When I was in the lab today I heard one of my colleagues talking about a bet that she took when she was in college."

"A bet?" Jonah asked.

He took clothes out of the wardrobe and dressed as she

continued to flip through the pages of the book, her eyes now scanning the text frantically as if she were desperately looking for something specific in the words. Aubrey nodded.

"Yeah. Apparently she and some of the people in one of her classes were having a study group. They had been learning about innovations and specific applications, and one of them started talking about an old factory that he had heard of when he was younger. They had been studying for hours and getting a little delirious and one of them bet that the others wouldn't go into the factory."

"Why?" Jonah asked.

He knew that his voice was holding more tension than he wanted it to, but the emotion that was inside him was tightening in his chest and aching in his belly, making him feel pulled and pressured like what was happening around him was becoming too much.

"There were all these stories about what used to happen inside that factory."

"Like things being manufactured?"

Aubrey looked up at him and he could see mild surprise in her eyes.

"Are you upset about something?" she asked.

Jonah shook his head.

"No. Just keep going. What were they saying about the factory?"

"It seemed that no one actually knew what was going on in that factory. They knew what was made in it, but even that was still just from records. They didn't know what the stuff was for or why it was made. The company made it for a while and then one day everything and everyone was just gone. The factory went from busy to abandoned seemingly overnight. Can you make a guess what they were making?"

She looked at him with a glint of mischief in her eyes.

"Izalux," Jonah said, realization trickling into the back of his mind.

Aubrey nodded.

"They didn't have any idea what it was for, but they knew that the Orion Corporation owned that factory and then suddenly they were gone. There all kinds of myths and stories about what used to happen in the factory even before it was abandoned, but especially after."

"Like what?"

He walked up to the window seat and sat on the edge."

"They said that there would be strange sounds and flickers of light coming through the windows. Dark shadows. Voices. It was like it was haunted. So they bet that the girls wouldn't go into the factory and spend a night there."

"What happened to them?"

"I didn't catch the whole story because they moved to another section of the lab, but from what I got, they broke into the factory and found rooms that looked like they hadn't been touched in decades and then others that looked like they were still in use. There were bottles of Izalux everywhere, most of them empty. What was most interesting to me, though, was that she said they found a room that was painted completely black. Floor, ceiling, walls. Everything. It was just a huge black room. In the middle of the room were a bunch of cushions on the floor."

"What could that be?" Jonah asked.

Aubrey shook her head.

"I don't know. That was all that I heard."

"So that's what got you out of the bath that I made for you?" he asked. "Some woman in that lab of yours went into an old factory and was scared by a room that she didn't understand?"

Aubrey blinked a few times, her lips parted.

"I thought that you would understand," she said. "It's not just any factory. It's the Orion Corporation factory. The one that made the Izalux. The stories about strange things happening there confirm that there's more to this stuff than we know."

"Didn't we already know that?" Jonah asked. "I thought that was the whole point of all of this. We have no idea what it is, what it's used for, or why there are bottles of it in the medical ward. Did you really need some campfire ghost story to tell you that?"

Aubrey put the book down beside her and stood up to face him.

"What is wrong with you?" she asked. "Is this all because of the bath? I appreciate it that you did that for me. It was really sweet, but..."

"It's not the bath," Jonah said. "It was just that that was one of a string of things. All you think about is this project that you are doing at work."

"That's not true, Jonah." She looked down at herself and shook her head with a sigh of exasperation. "Wait a minute. I'm not going to have this conversation with you while I'm wearing a towel."

She pushed past him and went to the wardrobe to pull out clothes. Turning her back to him, she dressed quickly and then came back to the window where he stood.

"I've been watching you every day and it seems like you are getting more and more stressed. Every day you come home more tired and more frustrated."

"It's my work," Aubrey said, as if that excused what he saw on her face every time that she came home. "This is what I've aspired to the entire time that I was in school and throughout my entire career. It's an honor that I was chosen for this project, and I would have hoped that you would be proud of me for what I've accomplished."

"I *am* proud of you," he said, stepping up to her and taking her hands in his. "I am so proud of you. What you are doing is amazing, but that doesn't mean that I like what it's doing to you. You used to be so excited talking about your work and now there's no life in your eyes. I'm worried about you. This project has completely taken over your life."

"Are you only saying that because it means that I don't have as much energy and attention to spend on your project?" she asked angrily. "Because right this moment I am researching to help you. I do everything to help you."

"I know that," Jonah said. "I know that you have done so much for me and I can't imagine trying to do this without you. The thought of doing anything without you is awful for me. That's why I'm so upset. You're my wife, Aubrey. I love you with everything that's in me and I don't want to see you going through so much stress and anxiety because of this one project, a project that only matters to you because it is being done in the laboratory you always wanted to work in. I want to see you doing something that you really care about."

"I love you, too, Jonah," she said, her eyes softening. "I know that you're worried about me, but you don't need to be. This isn't like what we are researching for you. Just because Ryan is insane doesn't mean that all of the scientists that are at the laboratory are doing horrible thing with their work."

"Are you sure about that?" he asked.

Aubrey looked at him with a slight smile on her lips.

"Because you are a scientist," she said. "Things are different now. We have a newer facility and have a different focus for our work, but you are still a scientist who worked at the University. You didn't do anything terrible. You never had plans for taking over the Universe or breeding new combinations of species, did you?"

"That was a long time ago," Jonah said. "I was working in that University more than 115 years ago. The focus of the research and the facilities have changed, just like you said. How can I know that that's not all that changed? What if you are the only scientist who hasn't been corrupted like Ryan?"

"Don't you think that there would be more awareness of the horrible things that he's been doing if all of the people in the lab knew about them, or was in on them? Why would he need such a secretive facility and to make up stories about most of his work if he was just going along with what the rest of the lab was doing? Besides, there's a scientist who went to Uoria recently. Do you know George?"

"You know George?" Jonah asked, surprised by the revelation.

"Of course," Aubrey said. "He's one of the premier scientists in the University. His plans to go to Uoria to study the Denynso were hugely publicized. Do you think that he would have been that public and open about his plans to go there if he had some sort of nefarious plan attached to it?"

"Ryan sent Eden," Jonah pointed out.

"But even you admitted that no one knew about that. He wasn't a part of the exchange program and he never gave anyone full information about what she was meant to do there, because most people didn't even know that she was. George was very open about his plans. He even gave lectures before he went about what he was planning on doing there and the hopes that he had for the continued cooperation and alliance between the Denynso and Earth." She hesitated and then tilted her head at him. "How do you know George?"

Jonah sat down on the foot of the bed. The time had come for her to know more about him and what had really happened to him in the time that he spent on Uoria.

"You know that I was locked in place in the settlement on Uoria," he started.

"Yes," Aubrey said, coming to the bed and sitting beside him. "The Covra attacked and used a toxin to suspend all of you so that they could use you to incubate their young."

Jonah nodded.

"Right. Well, when the Denynso found us there, they didn't know what had happened to us, or what they could do to help us. They were essentially guarding us while they tried to figure out what happened and if there was anything that they could do. Once they realized that it had to do with the Covra, they reached out to those who were still at the compound and were working on a solution. George was there. So was his assistant."

"Ivy?" Aubrey asked.

"Yes. She apparently wasn't supposed to be there, but had shown up. George wasn't very happy about it, but we all ended up being glad that she was there. They finally realized that it took a human voice to break through the lock that the Covra put on us. The Covra hate human voices and are vulnerable to them. The Denynso voices were close and that was what helped them to fend the Covra off enough that they could get to us, but it took a real human voice to free us."

"Are there still people there on Uoria?" Aubrey asked.

"Absolutely," Jonah said. "Very few of us left the settlement to be with the Denynso and Mikana. When we created the settlement, it wasn't long before a lot of the crew just resigned themselves to the reality that we were going to be on Uoria for the rest of our lives. Our communication systems were destroyed, our ship was crashed beyond repair. Our pilot was dead. We knew that no one on Earth knew where we had ended up because it wasn't even a planet that we knew of at the time. They completely lost hope. But that also meant that they settled in and started creating a life there. Some of them were already in relationships or married, and others followed and got married. They started having children. There are some children there now who are getting into their teenage years. They don't know anything but Uoria and would probably never want to leave. They have their home there. Their families. Everything that we need, we make or do within the settlement. We have school for the children. The adults use their own skills to handle other needs of the people, like gardening, foraging, baking, making clothes, building homes. Back before the Covra we had a close alliance with the Mikana and utilized some of their skills to help us establish orchards and patches of both native crops and Earth plants that we grew with seeds we brought with us when we left."

"Why did you bring Earth seeds with you?" Aubrey asked. "You thought that you were just seeking out an illegal prison colony and working to free the prisoners if they were there."

Jonah opened his mouth and then closed it again. It wasn't a question that he had ever really pondered.

"There were certain supplies that we always had with us. I suppose that seeds might have been a part of them."

"But you don't know for sure?"

"I know that the teams that were going out into Far Space and had the potential of colonizing new planets or moons would carry seeds with them along with their food supplies to make sure that even if they got stuck for longer than they expected, they would have access to additional food supplies. They also sometimes offered seeds to other species so that they could grow the crops on their own planets."

"But you don't know if you usually had seeds for your kind of mission?" Aubrey asked.

Jonah narrowed his eyes at her.

"Why does this matter to you so much?" he asked. "Is there something suspicious about us having seeds to plant when we were on Uoria?"

"Well, yes," Aubrey said. "Doesn't it seem strange to you that you weren't planning on being on Penthos for any length of time, yet someone packed so much food as well as seeds for food crops?"

Buzzing started in his ears and Jonah felt like his vision was closing in slightly.

"What are you saying?" he asked.

"I don't know," she told him. "I don't know if I'm saying anything at all. It could be something completely normal. I'll be the first to admit that I have never gone on a mission like you have. I've never left Earth, so I don't know what would be normal to bring with you on a quest like you were going on when you first left for Penthos. There's just something about it that seems strange to me. It almost seems..." her voice faded and she shook her head. "Never mind."

"It almost seems like what?" Jonah asked.

Aubrey hesitated, seeming to search his face for indication of what he was thinking and feeling, as though it would influence what she was going to say to him.

"It almost seems like someone put them there on purpose. Like someone might have known that you weren't going to be gone for as short a time as you thought that you were going to be, or that you may end up somewhere where you were going to need the seeds."

"Who would do that?" he asked.

Aubrey shook her head.

"I don't know," she said again. He looked down at his lap, feeling the angry tension building up in him again. "Do you ever get homesick?"

The question startled Jonah and he looked up at her sharply.

"Homesick?" he asked. "What do you mean?"

"Do you ever miss the settlement on Uoria? You were there for a long time. Do you ever wish that you were there?"

Jonah wasn't sure how to respond. He thought about it for a few moments.

"I haven't really had much chance to think about that," he said. "I'm guessing that there will be a time when I do miss it. Like you said, I was there for a long time. It was my home. Even though I was never one of the ones who was convinced that we were always going to be there."

"What do you mean?"

"Even from the beginning, I didn't want to just give up. I wasn't resigned to the fact that we didn't have anything left. I wanted to get off of Uoria so much. I wanted to be back here where we could figure out exactly what happened and ensure that those responsible got what they deserved. I always felt like there was so much more that we could do. That I could do. That's why Rain and I spent so much time designing the vehicle that we brought here. It took years and there were plenty of times that I didn't think that it was actually going to work. But I couldn't give up. It was like as long as I was working on it, there was a chance. Even if that vehicle wasn't going to work out, as long as I was doing something, anything, I wasn't giving up and I was ensuring that one day I was going to be back on Earth."

"Is that how Rain felt about it, too?"

Jonah could hear the slant in Aubrey's voice, like she was trying to sound casual but the faint touches of jealousy and nervousness in her voice were breaking through the façade.

"I think so," he said. "She and I had been friends for a long time, but it wasn't like we spent huge amounts of time talking about our feelings or anything."

"You didn't?" she asked.

Jonah shook his head.

"No. We talked a couple of times about how it seemed like everyone else had given up and that we still wanted to find a way to go back to Earth. We were angry while the rest chose to be sad. They were longing for the memories of Earth and what they felt like they had already lost. We still believed that there was a chance that we could get back and keep working on the mission that we had started with. We didn't want to lose anything. We wanted the careers that we had spent so much of our lives studying, training, and preparing for."

"When you were thinking about everything that you had left behind on Earth and everything that you might not be able to have if you didn't get back, was a family ever something that you thought about?"

"My family?" Jonah asked.

"A family that you didn't have yet," Aubrey clarified. "Did you ever think that being on Uoria for the rest of your life would mean that you wouldn't get married or have children?" She glanced down uncomfortably and then back at him. "Or was there someone on the settlement that you might have been interested in having a life with if you didn't ever get a chance to leave?"

Jonah held her hands tightly and stared into her eyes, trying without saying anything directly to reassure her that she was everything to him and that there was nothing for her to be jealous about.

"I had plenty of time to choose someone else. If I had wanted to, I would have. But there was never a time when I was on that settlement that I even thought for a second about getting married or having a family."

"And now?" she asked.

"Well," Jonah said with a grin as he lifted her hand and kissed her ring, "I think that I've already answered the question about getting married."

"And having a family?" Aubrey asked. "Is that something that you've ever thought about?"

She looked suddenly smaller, more fragile and vulnerable. Jonah didn't know what to say. He didn't want to hurt her, but he also didn't have the right words to answer her properly.

"I don't know what to say to you that would be an honest answer. I don't know where life is going to take me. Us. Right now all I know is that I have you and that is more than I ever could have hoped to have had. The rest is something that I will have to figure out as the time comes. One step at a time."

7

———

Rain stood at the window of her former bedroom and stared out over the settlement. She remembered the first time that she had stood in that room, more than a year after they crashed on Uoria. Up until then they had lived in small, temporary shelters that they were able to cobble together. Some had tried to piece together blankets and other fabric from the crash to make tents, but they were quickly found to be inadequate. Over time they had collected more of the remnants from the crash and gathered resources from the surrounding planet to help them make more permanent structures. Out of the salvage of the StarCity rose a village, and they surrounded it with a stone wall like the one that they had seen at the kingdom of the nearby Mikana. It gave them a sense of permanence, anchoring them on the planet that was now what most of them considered to be their home.

It was a wonderful feeling to have a more permanent home in the settlement after spending so much time hunkering in shelters that barely protected her from the unpredictable and sometimes brutal elements of the new planet. At the same time, however, there was a strange sense of forced happiness that hung over the building. She knew that there were some members of the crew who were thrilled that the skeletons of the settlement were finally fleshing out and building into homes, gathering places, shops, and other buildings that made them feel more like they weren't just floating, hovering somewhere in space, but truly secured to this frontier. Rain, though, wasn't as jubilant. This place still didn't feel like home. She felt like nothing more than a visitor there, borrowing the time, the space, even the very air that she was breathing, from the natives of Uoria. She was surrounded by what was left of their time on Earth and it made her feel as though everyone else in the crew was trying to recreate it, pretend that the salvaged pieces had never been a ship, almost as though they had always been there. Over time, she had become more accustomed to the space, even found herself enjoying the peace and comfort of a room that belonged entirely to her rather than having a bunkmate and feeling as though she was never really alone. But it had never taken away the longing for Earth. She had never resigned herself to this reality or given up her dream of one day returning to her home and completing the goals that she had made for herself.

Rain still hadn't given herself over to the settlement in the way that the rest had and she knew that she never would. She looked down at those who still had a spark of adventure and a desire for justice within them gathering in the street beneath her. It had been more than two days since she had arrived back at the settlement to ask for the help of those who were willing to go back to the Mikana kingdom and then on to Penthos with her, and finally they were nearly ready to leave. Those who were going with her had bags sitting around their feet and weapons strapped to their backs. Some had their partners with them, others were clinging to them, saying goodbye. These all held the false smiles, the air of dismissiveness as they pretended that the weight that was pushing down on all of them wasn't there. They pretended that when they said goodbye it was only for a short time, just a brief jaunt just as they had planned for their first visit to Penthos. In the backs of their eyes, though, she could see the pain of knowledge. She could see that they knew that it was very likely that many of them would never set foot on this planet again, and that when they stopped touching their loved ones to journey to the kingdom, it would be the final time that they would feel the touch of those people.

Rain stepped back and looked around her room again. She didn't have any of the falseness in her heart. She had the strong sense within her that when she walked out of the settlement to return to Penthos, those fleeting final moments would be the last time that she would see this place, that she might never come back. There was unexpected sadness in that feeling. She had been wanting to get out of the settlement and back to Earth for as long as she had been there, yet this place represented so much to her. This is where they had been through some of the most difficult parts of their lives and prevailed. This was where they learned that they were far stronger than they had ever known that they were and could overcome things that they never even knew existed. This was a place that would always be indescribably impactful to her. But had been stuck. She had been trapped here and was beyond ready to put it behind her. This was her chance for freedom and to finally break free of the control that the Covra had tried to hold over them once and for all.

Below her she saw a man hug his brother and then step back, his hand reaching down to envelope the tiny hand of his child who stood beside him. The little girl had glossy curls that hung to her shoulders and the eyes of her mother. Rain remembered them before they left Earth. They barely knew each other then. Now they had built a family and neither wanted to leave Uoria. An involuntary thought ran through Rain's mind and she wondered if perhaps she was wrong about never seeing this place again and if there would be some day when she would bring her children there to see the settlement and learn about her past.

The thought brought emotion to Rain's throat and she fought tears that stung in the bottoms of her eyes. This was a challenging thought for her. When she was younger, she had always assumed that she would one day have a family. Once the days of her missions were over and she had accomplished all that she thought that she was going to, she would find someone to love, get married, and have children. It was what was expected of her and something that she never questioned. That all changed when they got to Uoria, however. No longer did she think of a future with anything more than herself. She had too much else on her mind to even ponder the potential of finding someone to love or one day being responsible for the lives of children. There were moments when she barely felt that she could handle the responsibility of her own life.

Then she met Lynx. Everything changed. So much more than she ever thought that it could. So much more than she even knew until now. Suddenly she could imagine having a family again. Part of her that had been hiding away for so long was open and alive again, and this filled her with a new sense of resolve. This had to be done. Wherever it took her and whatever she had to do, she wasn't just fighting for what had happened, but also for what could have been, and what still may be.

Rain gathered her bags and rushed out of the room, closing the door behind her before running down the stairs and out into the crowd.

"Rain," one of the men said as she approached. "How many people can you fit on the vehicle that you brought with you from the kingdom?"

The realization sank in and Rain realized the tremendous gap in her planning. She had taken the vehicle because it would bring her to the settlement far more quickly than walking, and she didn't want to waste any time. She hadn't thought about who might be coming back with her, and now she realized that far more of the men from the settlement and even some of the women were primed and ready to go along with her, but she didn't know how to transport them back to the kingdom efficiently. She looked to the man who had spoken.

"I can bring a few on the vehicle with me," she said. "The rest of you wait here. When we get to the kingdom we will get other vehicles and return for the rest of you."

Part of her expected that they would protest, but instead, they nodded and several stepped forward, offering themselves to go along with her on this first leg of the journey. She helped them to put their belongings into the vehicle and then climb aboard before assuring the rest still standing in the center of the street that they would soon be back for them. She started the vehicle and they headed out, going toward the kingdom as fast as they could.

8

I vy closed the door to the infirmary as carefully as she could, not wanting to wake any of the injured that might be resting. Nylek was sitting up in his bed, one hand holding Mina's hand while the other grasped a piece of fruit. He smiled at her as she approached.

"Hi," she said, resting her hand on Mina's shoulder. "How are you feeling today, Nylek?"

"Much better," he admitted. "I wish that one of the healers was here so that they could do a full healing and I could be done with this, but I'm just grateful for the supplies that Ciyrs left with us and the efforts of the doctor here. I really didn't think that I was going to survive that."

Ivy smiled at him.

"You did fine," she said. "You're strong. There's nothing that a little hybrid army can do to you."

Nylek laughed.

"I'm so glad that you have so much faith in me," he said. "But it seems like those hybrids were fairly good at doing something to me when we were on Penthos."

"Not anymore," Ivy said. "We'll be ready when we get back."

"We?"

Ivy turned around at the sound of the familiar voice and saw Ellora standing in the doorway. Maxim's mother looked concerned and curious, and Ivy took a step toward her.

"Ellora," she started.

"Is it safe to assume that by 'we' you mean that you intend on going back to Penthos with the rest of us?"

As she had largely since they met, the Mikana woman sounded suspicious of Ivy, as if she thought that now that they were back on Uoria, she would take the opportunity to rush back to the Denynso compound and call for a shuttle from Earth. Ivy knew that the time had come to tell Ellora about the baby. Though she still felt hesitant to talk about it, and would have hesitated longer if she thought that she could, she knew that things weren't exactly what she thought that they were and that there was even more to what was going on than she thought. Now was the time when she needed to be honest with Ellora and tell her what was happening so that the older woman could finally understand her thoughts and believe that she was fully and utterly committed to Maxim and didn't want to return to Earth without him. Telling Ellora about the impending birth of her first grandchild would be a way for her to connect more closely with her and to give them, all of them, more motivation in the fight.

"Could I speak to you, Ellora?" Ivy asked. "I know that you're busy, but I need just a moment of privacy with you. There's something that I need to talk with you about."

Ellora nodded and Ivy looked down at Nylek with an apologetic, encouraging smile before starting out of the room. They exited the infirmary and made their way across the village toward Ellora's house. They walked along in silence, Ivy trying to bring to mind what she was going to say and how Ellora might react to the news.

Finally they arrived at Ellora's house and they settled onto a couch in the front room.

"Can I make you a cup of coffee?" Ellora asked.

The offer made Ivy remember the first time that she met Ellora. She had been so surprised to find out that this section of Uoria had a beverage that had come from coffee beans from Earth. The fact that they were able to grow the beans and create them into a hot, strong, bitter beverage was truly impressive to her, but it also just made her grateful for the deep swallows of a beverage that she often couldn't do without for more than half an hour when she was at home in the laboratory. Her mouth watered at the thought of the coffee, but she knew that she shouldn't drink it. She drew in a breath and shook her head.

"No, thank you," she said.

Ellora looked at her strangely and settled onto the couch beside her.

"Is something wrong?"

"Um," Ivy said, looking away as she tried to gather her words. She looked back up at her and shook her head. "No. Nothing's wrong. I just don't think that drinking coffee would be good for the baby."

It was blatant and rushed, no buildup, no preparation. It was the only way that she could bring herself to get the words out. She saw them pass through Ellora as if they didn't make any impact on her at all, and then her face started to change. The muscles tightened and her eyes widened slightly, not as though she were surprised, but almost as though she were trying to take in more of Ivy as she spoke. Her breath trembled in her throat as she drew it in.

"Baby?" she asked, her voice barely above a whisper.

Ivy nodded.

"Yes," she said.

"You are carrying my first grandchild?"

Ivy nodded again.

"I am," she said. "That's why I came back here to Uoria rather than staying on Penthos with Maxim. He wanted to make sure that I was safe and he wanted me to come see the midwives so I could find out about the pregnancy."

"What did you find out?" Ellora asked.

"I left the midwife before I was able to find out much. I didn't feel right being there by myself. This is all so new to me and I didn't know what to do. I didn't want to find out everything alone."

"Does anyone else know about the baby?"

"Only Rain," Ivy said. "Maxim didn't think that we should tell anybody while we were on Penthos. It would be too much of a distraction when they were facing the hybrids the first time. He thought that everybody would be too worried about me and the baby to concentrate on the fight there. I honestly think that that is a big part of why he sent me back here. He didn't want to think about me when he should be focusing on the fight."

Ivy felt an unexpected rush of emotion tighten in her throat and wished that she had allowed Ellora to make the coffee for her just so that she could have the comfort of holding the warm mug in her hands.

"My son is far too stubborn for his own good," Ellora said. "He should know that a baby would be a source of motivation. Everyone would want to know that they are fighting for the safety and the happiness of the future generation." She gave a soft laugh. "It reminds me of Aegeus when I first told him that I was carrying Maxim."

"He was worried about you?"

"There were days when I thought that he was never going to let me leave our bedroom. He was convinced that being pregnant somehow made me fragile and completely vulnerable to everything. I think that's just the way of men. They don't understand that it takes far more strength to carry and deliver a child than anything that many of them will do with their lives. Do you think that most of the men in Rey's court would be able to go through a pregnancy and bringing a baby into this world?"

Ivy couldn't help but laugh. From what little she knew about the court, they were not men who could even begin to be compared to the Mikana army or to the Denynso warriors. The King himself led the army, but the men in his court were there primarily to advise him when he needed it and to perform ambassador duties when Rey was not available. They were rarely seen and even more rarely in action.

"I wish that Maxim could see me as strong."

"He will," Ellora said. "He loves you. He just hasn't figured out that he can love you and want to protect you, and appreciate that you are able to take care of yourself and the baby within you at the same time." She looked out the window and then back at Ivy. "If you'd like, I can go back to the midwife with you. They might be able to tell you more about the baby. I know that you would rather have Maxim with you, but..."

"I would love for you to be there with me."

Ivy felt her heart swelling. Though she and Maxim's mother hadn't been close since they met, she felt some of the tension between them easing. She knew that it had been troublesome for Ellora to see her come back to Uoria rather than staying on Penthos to support Maxim, and now that she knew the reason behind it, she seemed far more willing to start to build a connection with her.

THE MIDWIFE SEEMED surprised to see her when she opened the door and saw Ivy standing in front of the office again. Ellora was standing close behind her and when the midwife saw her, she smiled.

"You've told Ellora the wonderful news?"

"She has."

"Congratulations."

"Thank you, Opaline. Ivy says that she left before she was able to get a full examination."

"She did," Opaline said. "I just assumed that she decided that she couldn't trust me since I'm not a doctor like they have on Earth."

Ivy shook her head.

"That's not it," she said. "Please believe me. I trust you. If Maxim and Ellora both say that you will be able to help me through this, then I am willing to trust you completely. I just didn't want to do this on my own."

"I understand," Opaline said, her face brightening slightly at the statement. "If you'd like, I'm still happy to examine you. I will still not be able to tell you everything, but I can tell you some."

"I'd like that."

Several minutes later Ivy was laying in the examination room, her hand grasping Ellora's as the midwife examined her. Finally Opaline stepped back and invited her to sit up. Ivy complied and pulled a blanket up around her, suddenly chilled and nervous about what the midwife was going to tell her. Until that moment she hadn't worried about the baby's health or anything that could go wrong in any pregnancy, but especially a pregnancy that was unprecedented among all of those who were available to help her.

"You are looking very healthy," Opaline said. "Your body is responding beautifully to the pregnancy and is beginning to prepare to bring this little baby into the world to meet all of us."

Ivy felt nervousness bubble into her chest.

"Already?" she asked. "I've only known a few weeks."

"It isn't imminent," Opaline said. "You still have time. But remember that a Mikana pregnancy is far faster than a human pregnancy. Our kind, most of the species on Uoria, come from ancestors who have had too much risk and danger around us to have the luxury of long pregnancies."

"I feel like my baby is far safer inside of me than out," Ivy said.

"I know," Opaline said. "I know that you feel that way. All mothers do. But a baby that has been born can be protected even when the mother can't. Your little one can be brought wherever it would be safest once it has been born, but if it is still within you, it can only be protected where you are. I know that you want to hold onto this little one for as long as you can. Every mother wants for the only thing that her baby hears is to be her voice and her heartbeat, but you must trust that the way that it is is the way that is best."

Ivy took another breath, trying to calm herself. She felt so much more protective toward her baby now that she had told Ellora about the pregnancy and taken the step of being examined by the midwife. Though she felt a strong link to it and already loved it, this had made it so much more real for her and the instincts within her had surged forward.

"When do you think the baby will come?" Ellora asked, the tone of her voice soft and soothing as though she were trying to gloss over the tension and keep the conversation moving forward on a more positive note. "Will it be soon?"

"I can't be sure," Opaline said. "There are still things about this pregnancy that are controlled by Ivy being human. From the signs that I see, though, this little one should come within the next two months." She reached out and brushed a lock of Ivy's hair away from her shoulder. "I am here to take care of you, Ivy. We're going to help you through this and will be here for you when the baby is born. Just relax now. Take care of yourself and your little one, and start preparing to hold it in your arms."

The midwife walked out of the room and Ivy brought her hands to her belly. All of the activity seemed to have woken the baby up and she ran her hands along the swell, feeling the little shifts and bumps of it moving within her.

"I wish I knew if it was a boy or girl," she said.

"You'll know soon enough," Ellora said.

Ivy smiled bigger than she had in as long as she could remember.

"I think that Maxim would probably want to have a son, but I would love to see him holding a little girl. I think that he would be an amazing father to a daughter."

"Why do you think that he would want a son?"

"He has a brother and he has admired his father so much. I think that he would be proud to have a son who could follow his legacy."

"I know that Maxim will be happy with whatever child is being given to him. He will be a wonderful father."

"I know." Ivy sighed and cradled her belly a little tighter. "I miss him so much. I'm so excited about the baby and I wish that he was here to be excited with me. Or that I was there with him."

"Would you want to go back to Penthos?" Ellora asked. "Even knowing the danger that is there now?"

Ivy nodded.

"Yes," she said. "I know that what is going on there is difficult and dangerous, but if Maxim is there, that is where I want to be. I promised him that I was going to stand beside him and that I was with him no matter what. I could have left Uoria whenever I wanted to, but I didn't. I stayed here because I know that what Maxim is facing is incredibly important to him, and what matters to him is what matters to me. I want to be wherever he is and helping him in any way that I can. I don't want to go through this pregnancy without him and I don't want him to go through this battle without me."

She expected Ellora to argue with her, to try to convince her that she should stay on Uoria under the care of Opaline. Instead, she gave a slow nod.

"Then I think that when the ship goes back to Penthos, you should come."

"What?" Ivy asked.

"I think that you should do whatever you think is right, Ivy. If you think that you should be on Penthos with Maxim, then that is what you should do."

"I thought that you would be really resistant to me doing anything that dangerous while I was pregnant. I assumed that you would tell me that I should stay here and just wait for him to come back."

"I have spent far too much of my life being too cautious," Ellora told her. "Especially after Aegeus left. I have resisted so many things that I thought of doing because I thought that they would be just too dangerous for me. Maybe if I hadn't, maybe if I followed my heart before now, I wouldn't have had to spend so much of my life without Aegeus."

Ellora smiled at her and then left the room to allow her to get dressed again. Ivy felt a wave of relief and excitement rush over her. Soon the army would be trained, they would have gathered all of the supplies that they would need for the journey and when they arrived on Penthos, they would be back on the ship, and she would be on her way back to Maxim.

9

———

Maxim watched as Eden wrapped his injured hand with a bandage. The warmth from the healing that she had administered was still making its way through his veins and he could already feel the ointments that she had placed over the cut taking away the pain.

"Do you have any other injuries?" she asked. "Anything else that I can heal for you?"

Maxim shook his head.

"No. I'm alright. I need to help the other men. They are in far worse condition than I am."

He climbed down off of the table that had been converted into a treatment bed and walked into the other room where some of the other men were being treated. A hybrid man sat on the floor, his back against the wall as he gripped a deep wound in his thigh. Blood bubbled up between his fingers and his eyes were closed against the pain, but he was making no sound. He was confused and nearly overwhelmed by the sudden presence of so many more people in the compound. Though he had been expecting the Denynso and some of the others that they had with them, he was taken off-guard by the strange species that were with them and the hybrids that they brought along with the wounded.

"Who is that?" he demanded, grabbing ahold of Gyyx's arm and gesturing toward the hybrid man.

"I don't know," Gyyx said. "They don't have names."

"They?"

"The hybrids that came from Earth with us," the warrior explained.

"I don't understand," Maxim said. "You brought some of the hybrid army with you?"

"They were where we found your father," Gyyx said. "They were in very bad condition."

"But weren't they fighting you there?"

"You need to talk to Pyra," Gyyx said. "He'll explain everything to you."

"I need to be here," Maxim protested. "I need to help the wounded."

"You've done enough. They are being well cared-for by Ciyrs, Elianna, and Eden. For now, you need to take care of yourself. Get something to eat. Rest."

Maxim nodded and backed out of the room. He knew that Gyyx was right. As much as he wanted to help take care of the wounded or to help those who had just arrived from Earth, he could feel the effects of days of not eating or sleeping enough starting to pull down on him. Though his mind felt like it was moving even faster than it had been when he was on the battlefield, his body was dragging and he knew that soon he wouldn't be able to do anything if he didn't stop to rest and eat.

The scent of rich, fulfilling food drew him from the

building across the open courtyard toward the flickering of the fires. The energy in this area of the compound was different. While the makeshift infirmary was tense, almost frantic, things were calmer and more relaxed here. People roamed around eating, gathered in tight groups to talk, and lay on the ground staring up at the stars. There was the clear sense of peacefulness here and Maxim spent a few moments just enjoying the feeling.

One of the women approached him and held out what looked like a large chunk of bread. He accepted it and saw that the center of the bread had been carved out and filled with thick stew. She had toasted the leftover bread and handed that to him by way of a spoon.

"I'm sorry," she said. "We ran out of utensils."

"It's alright," Maxim said. "This looks delicious. Thank you."

She offered a smile and walked away, returning to the fire to create another of the meals. He dipped the bread into the stew and took his first savory bite. The rich flavors ignited his hunger even further and Maxim hurried to eat more of the stew. He was taking the final bite of the gravy-soaked bread bowl when he turned and saw his father standing several yards away. He was staring at him without emotion, unmoving, as if he wasn't sure if he should approach him.

Suddenly Maxim didn't know how he was supposed to feel or what he was supposed to think. He was over-whelmed with emotion that he didn't know how to process. His chest felt like it was crushing and each breath was harder to draw into his lungs. He had to get away. He couldn't keep standing there, just wondering what either of them was supposed to do. Not paying attention to where he was going, Maxim started running. He needed to break out of the tension and get somewhere where he felt he could breathe.

Before he realized where he was, Maxim had run beyond the wall of the compound and was standing out in the dark sand away from the warmth and reassurance that the surrounding wall provided. He paused, trying to pull himself back under control. He hated feeling like this. He hated the sense that he couldn't manage his emotions and the thoughts that were running through his head. The feeling of someone behind him made him turn and he saw Aegeus approaching him.

"I always wondered how fast you would be when you grew up," he said.

Maxim's muscles tightened as his father's voice touched his ears for the first time since he was a small child.

"I guess you never thought that you would know," Maxim said.

"You're right," Aegeus told him. "I didn't." There was a high, chilling scream somewhere in the distance and Aegeus took another step closer. "You can't be out here, Maxim. It's too dangerous."

Maxim didn't understand why, but something snapped inside him and a rush of painful emotion filled his chest.

"Suddenly you want to be my father and worry about what's happening to me?"

He felt guilty as soon as the words came out of his mouth, but Maxim didn't know what to do. He looked away, his hands planted on his hips. Aegeus backed up a few steps and without saying anything, Maxim started following him. They walked back to the compound and Aegeus led him to a quiet place away from the busyness of the center courtyard. Maxim stood with his back against the wall of one of the empty buildings and stared ahead of him, not trusting himself to look at Aegeus. Several long, silent seconds passed between them before the older man spoke.

"Do you hate me?"

The words cut through Maxim and his eyes closed against them. His head hung and he shook it.

"No," he said. "Of course I don't hate you. I couldn't hate you. I just don't know what I'm supposed to think or do." He finally brought himself to turn and look at him. "I've been waiting for this moment for so long. Even when I thought that you were dead, I dreamed of what it would be like if I got to see you again. What I would do. What I would say. I always had so much that I wanted to tell you. Now that it's finally here, though, I don't know how I'm supposed to handle it."

"What do you mean?" Aegeus asked. "It's just me. I know it's been a long time and that you had to grow up without me, and I'm so sorry for that, but I'm still your papa."

Maxim slid down the wall so that he sat in the warm sand. He pulled his knees up and rested his arms on them.

"I'm worried that you will be disappointed in me," he admitted. "Or that you will think that I haven't done what I should have in life. I never got to know everything that you dreamed of for me, or who you wanted me to be, and I don't know if I lived up to any of it."

Aegeus shook his head.

"Maxim, there is nothing that you could do that would make me disappointed in you. I never wanted anything more from you than for you to be yourself and to be a good man. I can see that you are. I've heard what these other men say about you and the way they look when they talk about you. It is obvious that they trust and respect you. How could I ever not think that you aren't everything that I could ever want for my son?" He hesitated. "I'm worried that you will be disappointed in me."

"How could I be disappointed in you?" Maxim asked.

"I was captured when you were so young. Any memories that you might have of me are through the lens of a child. I can't possibly live up to what you thought of me. Especially now that you know what I went through."

Maxim tilted his head.

"All I know is that Ryan held you captive in the laboratory on Earth. I don't know anything else."

Aegeus looked pained, as though there was something that he didn't want to admit to Maxim but he knew that he didn't have a choice.

"I was Klimnu, Maxim," he said. "He held me for a time and then he mutated me and I've been Klimnu for several years."

"Fully Klimnu?" Maxim asked.

"As much as he was able to change me," Aegeus said. "He couldn't change my heart or my mind, but he totally changed my body. I spent more of the time that I have been away from you as that horrifying creature than I spent as I was before I left. The only reason that I am this way again is because of the efforts of the Denynso healers. Even though I look like this again, though, I know what I've been. I'm worried that now that you know, you, your brother, and your mother won't be able to look at me the same way, much less be able to love me."

Maxim hated the look of pain on his father's face and the slight tremor in his voice as he spoke. He knew now more than he had before that his father being away from him wasn't his choice. He had been trapped in a way that was far more severe than just the captivity of his body. Maxim stood and stepped up closer to his father so that he could see his face in the pale light of the moon. His face was different. It was worn and tired, and the years had etched themselves across his skin in lines around his eyes and the corners of his mouth. None of it mattered, though. This was still his father. Still the man he had always wished that he would see again.

"I still see the father that I saw when I was a child. You are no different than the man I said goodbye to that last day. Nothing that you went through is your fault."

"Thank you," Aegeus said.

He hesitated and then opened his arms to Maxim. Maxim stepped into them and felt his father gather him close.

"Papa," he whispered.

"My son," Aegeus whispered back. "My son." He took Maxim by his shoulders and guided him back, looking into his eyes. "Where is your brother? Is he here with you?"

Maxim shook his head.

"No. He was wounded before the rest of you got here and had to be brought back to Uoria with some of the crew."

"Is he alright?"

"I'm sure he is. He was doing well when he left. I just wanted to make sure that he got the treatment that he needed. It's too dangerous for him here."

"And your mother?" Aegeus asked.

His voice sounded like the question was painful to ask, but Maxim completely understood. He couldn't imagine what it would be like if he was kept from Ivy for so many years and finally had the opportunity to potentially be with her again. There would be so much fear and anxiety that would keep him from being entirely happy about the situation.

"She's fine," Maxim said. "She has been. At least, as much as anyone could expect."

"Has she..." his voice trailed off.

"She hasn't remarried," Maxim said quickly, wanting to reassure him. "She never forgot about you. I promise that she has thought of you every single day since the day that you left."

"And I've thought of all of you."

10

"Every time that we come here I feel more and more like we shouldn't be here," Aubrey whispered as they crept through the door and into the abandoned waiting room of the medical ward.

"Which is precisely why I think that this is the exact place that we are supposed to be," Jonah replied. "Besides, it was your idea."

"It was not my idea to come back here," Aubrey said. "I just said that we should consider going to the Izalux factory and having a look around. You're the one who took it from that point to us coming back here again."

"I told you, I think that we need to get the patient records from the reception room before we go to the factory."

"Yes, I know. But why? What are those patient records going to tell you that we don't already know? We've gone over your record and all of the records for all of the people who were on the Nyx 23 crew. We have those records back at home. Why do we need the records for any of the other people who might have come in here for treatment? Especially before we go to the factory? And how do you even know that they are still here? Aren't those records something that they would want to take with them when they are transferring into another medical facility? I mean, I know that they didn't take their equipment or furniture or anything, but I can almost understand that. But records? If they are starting another medical facility just on the other side of the campus, wouldn't they need those to keep seeing their regular patients?"

"You would think," Jonah said. "But keep in mind that this facility was supposed to be destroyed. Them leaving the equipment and the furniture in it wasn't something that was planned. Whoever made the decision to keep this ward rather than getting it torn down like originally planned made the decision to keep these things in it. Somewhere along the line the patient records for Nyx 23 were taken and brought down into the basement. All except for mine. Mine stayed here. No one ever thought about the fact that they didn't see our records again. But you're right. If they were going to keep up with their regular patients, they would need to have their records when they moved over to the new ward. So if we do find other records, it means that someone didn't want anybody else thinking about the fact that those people came into this ward."

"I don't think that I'm following you."

Jonah started across the waiting room toward what used to be the reception window. He rested his hands on the counter, a memory flashing through his mind of the last time that he had stood there. It had been so completely mundane, nothing that he would ever give a second thought because of every time that he had done the exact same thing throughout his time at the University. It was just another step. Another part of the preparation for this mission. That morning had been nothing unusual, nothing out of the ordinary of his day-to-day life. Jonah could remember eating breakfast with some friends, then taking a run around campus. He had gotten into a conversation with one of his colleagues and was nearly late for his appointment. When he arrived, he had stood right in this spot and apologized to the receptionist, who reassured him that getting to the appointment a few minutes before the scheduled time was still acceptable. The thought made Jonah laugh. He had always been so particular about time, reinforced in his scientific work that every second mattered.

"Your friend said that there were stories about the factory being haunted because there were sounds and people moving around in there. Then when your friend actually went in there, they found that strange room that they thought was some sort of ritual space."

"Right. But that was just a few years ago. This place closed down a century ago."

"We've already established that the Orion Corporation has been around for a long time. Just look at the labels of the bottles. They were making Izalux right around the time when the medical ward closed down. That factory was in action then. So what if it was in action before Nyx 23 left and in the years right after before they closed the ward? We already know that there has to be some kind of link between the Izalux and Nyx 23. What if it went beyond that? What if the factory was more than a factory?"

"I still don't understand what that would have to do with the patient records."

Jonah approached the door that led behind the reception counter and tried the doorknob. It was locked, but the thin wooden door gave way easily to one strong kick. They stepped into the office area and he saw rows of file cabinets, their drawers standing open.

"The records that the University kept were different from those kept by other hospitals and medical facilities at the time. They used computers that held all of the records for everyone. Medical teams could access them through any computer or device that they wanted to, but there was a tremendous security breach a few years before I entered the University."

"A security breach?" Aubrey asked.

Jonah nodded as he approached one of the files and looked into the top drawer. Finding it empty, he closed it and looked into the next.

"It was considered an act of terrorist aggression at the time, but they weren't ever able to identify exactly who did it. I'm surprised that you didn't learn about it in school. The medical information for millions of people was accessed and compromised. Hundreds of thousands of people endured unnecessary procedures and were given the wrong medications or treatments. Many died and countless others were damaged in ways that impacted them for the rest of their lives."

He glanced back at Aubrey and she looked as though something had just occurred to her.

"We did learn about something like that," she said, "but all they told us was that there as widespread chaos, illness, and death as a result of a plague."

"A plague?" Jonah asked. "That's an interesting way to describe it. I suppose it makes sense, though. It's the same reason that the University changed their medical records."

"Why?" Aubrey asked.

"Panic," Jonah said. "Everyone relies so much on things that they can't see. They like to just believe that everything is happening the way that they think that it should. They put their trust into the unknown and if they didn't think that it was going to work, it would drive them mad. Even when people figured out what was happening and started to fix it, there were people who tried to pretend that it wasn't happening. The media went from sensationalizing the entire situation to totally glossing over it to going to great extents to reassure everyone that the danger was over and everything had been fixed."

"But the University?"

"From then the lack of trust for larger technology and information sharing became integrated into nearly everything that the University did, particularly at the medical facility. Rather than keeping medical records for the patients that came here in a large computer system accessible by essentially anyone, each patient was given an individual, separate file not linked to anything or anyone else. It was similar to records from generations ago, when the information was kept on paper and stored in individual folders. There was no way to access that information unless you had that particular file. The University devised the type of files that you saw. Both computerized and individual. That meant that all of the information in them was completely secure, known only by the medical team that had been authorized to interact with that specific patient. That eliminated the risk of any tampering and ensured that no one could access it without permission."

"But your file was tampered with," Aubrey said.

"Exactly," Jonah said. "That means that the doctor who handled our examinations that day was either a part of whatever was going to happen…"

"Or someone found your files later and used authorization to change them after the fact."

"Right. But that means that the files themselves were part of the ruse all along, right up until we didn't come back to Earth. Then we disappeared. They didn't need our files anymore. But they also didn't want anyone finding them at the new facility and noticing the discrepancies. That's why they stayed here. Just because the Izalux has something to do with Nyx 23 doesn't mean that that is the only strand of events. What if Nyx 23 wasn't the beginning? What if there are other things that are connected, that could explain more of what all of this means? If that's the case, then any other patient records that might still be here wouldn't necessarily have to do with the crew. They could be linked to the factory and to all of this in another way."

Jonah moved on to another of the file cabinets and closed the drawers one by one as he found them empty.

"Have I told you recently how amazing you are?"

He turned to look at Aubrey and smiled.

"No," he said.

She smiled at him and took a few steps toward him.

"Well, you are. You are completely amazing. And I'm sorry for our fight yesterday."

Jonah stood and closed the space between them.

"That wasn't a fight. Was it?"

"I think so," Aubrey said, nodding. "But it was my fault. You're right. I have gotten totally wrapped up in this project at work and between that and this, I've lost all focus on everything else, even you, and that's not alright."

"It's my fault, too," Jonah said. "I know that you've worked so hard to get to where you are in your career. That shouldn't change just because I came along. I am incredibly proud of you and shouldn't put so much pressure on you. Especially when it comes to all of this. I'm the one who got obsessed with this and decided to keep looking into it."

"Of course you did," Aubrey said. "Anyone in your situation would. This isn't just your fight, Jonah. It's mine, too. I'm your wife and there are days when I need to remind myself just how lucky I am that you are my husband."

"I am far luckier than you are," Jonah said, reaching out and wrapping his arms around her waist.

"I don't think so," Aubrey said. "I don't know any other women who come home from a long day at work to find that their husband has made a bath for them just because he wants to make her happy."

"Well, if you did, I doubt that any of them would have been so willing to share with their husbands. They would have kept all of the bubbles for themselves."

Aubrey smiled and pressed closer to him.

"I would never be so selfish with my bubbles," she said. Her eyes took on a mischievous glint. "That reminds me. I believe that I got distracted right in the middle of something very important."

Jonah licked his lips.

"You're right," he said, starting to guide her back toward the desk. "I think that we have some very important unfinished business that we need to attend to."

Tightening his hands around her waist, Jonah lifted Aubrey from her feet and perched her on the edge of the desk. Taking the light that he wore around his neck off and placing it aside, he leaned forward and caught her mouth in a passionate kiss. He didn't want to hesitate. Though the way that he had touched her in their shared bath had been slow and exploratory, he didn't feel that he had that control at this moment. He desired her with a depth and a ferocity that went beyond anything that he ever could have imagined, and it only seemed to intensify with every passing day of their marriage. She comforted him and made him feel alive, soothed him and reaffirmed the motivation and drive that he had for every day.

Aubrey returned the passion that he showed her, parting her lips to welcome his tongue into her mouth and moaning softly when he parted her legs and stepped up between them. She pressed her hips forward and he felt the warmth of her body seeping through the thin panties that she wore beneath her skirt. His hands slid up her thighs, running along either side of her legs until they reached the waistband of her panties and began to draw them down. Aubrey lifted her hips so that he could remove them and Jonah dropped them to the floor before lowering himself to his knees in front of her.

In one swift movement Jonah lifted her legs up and draped them over his shoulders. The position opened her to him and he pushed her skirt up so that it pooled around her hips, revealing her sweet, ready core. Jonah groaned and dipped his head forward to run his tongue up though her folds. The warmth wetness of her rolled over his tongue and he eagerly lapped it up into his mouth. Aubrey cried out and parted her thighs further as she leaned back against the wall to support herself. As Jonah continued to explore her with his tongue, he lowered one hand from her leg to bring it to the front of his pants. His fully engorged cock sprang free as soon as he released the button and drew his zipper down, and Jonah wrapped his hand firmly around it. He felt Aubrey's fingers dig into his hair and knew that she was losing herself in the pleasure that he was giving her.

Jonah stroked himself in the same rhythm that he licked her and quickly felt the sensations spiraling upward until he nearly felt like he was losing control. Aubrey's body was opening to him, becoming wetter and softer the more attention that he lavished on her, and soon he couldn't hold off any longer. Climbing to his feet and letting her legs drop away from his shoulders, Jonah wrapped one arm around her hips and pulled her forward so that she nearly fell off of the edge of the desk. He caught her just before she slipped off and plunged into her in one swift movement. His head fell back and he groaned loudly at the feeling of her walls closing in around his erection like they had around his fingers. He didn't pause but started rolling his hips, thrusting further and further into her as Aubrey reached behind herself to rest on her hands. The support allowed Jonah to increase the speed and intensity of his thrusts and he opened his mouth to allow the stream of gasps and moans to escape unfettered.

In the light glowing up from where he had placed it on the desk Jonah could see Aubrey reclined in front of him. Even though she was fully dressed, something about her body being concealed was even more exciting to him. This was so much like their first time together, the impulsive, hurried decision that both brought them together and nearly tore them apart. Thinking about the overwhelming need he had had for her from the first moment that he saw her and the desperation that he had felt when he thought that he was never going to see her again peaked his arousal and he slammed into her. His cock throbbed with so much intensity it was almost painful and he dug his fingers into Aubrey's hips to balance the sensation.

Aubrey sat up suddenly and reached forward to wrap one hand around the back of Jonah's neck. Holding onto him tightly, she brought her other hand around and dipped it between her thighs. Jonah watched breathlessly as she ran her fingertips over her tightened pearl. After a few seconds she cried out and he felt the delicious tightening of her body around his, drawing him deeper into her and milking him with a frantic cascade of spasms.

A few moments later they held each other breathlessly, kissing along sweaty skin as they simply allowed the pleasure of their slowly waning climaxes to wash over them. He was thankful that they had waited until late into the night as they usually did to come down into the medical ward. It meant that there was less of a chance that there was anyone inside the laboratory to hear them. He knew that eventually they would have to reveal the presence of this section of the building and everything that they had discovered, but this was not the time. There was so much more that they needed to do, and as soon as they told anyone on Earth, he would no longer have the opportunity to do it.

Jonah gently withdrew from her and helped her down from the desk. He looked around at the floor to find her panties, and when he did, he leaned down to pick them up. As he was straightening, he noticed the bottom drawer of one of the file cabinets was not as far open as the others. He grasped the handle and pulled it open, gasping when he saw the stack of patient records inside. He took hold of a handful of them and stood, turning to Aubrey to show her what he had discovered.

Aubrey lifted the light so that they could see better as Jonah rested the records onto the desk. He scanned through them, trying to recognize some of the names that were engraved on the front of the computerized files. Some of them sounded vaguely familiar, but he couldn't place them. He was nearly to the bottom of the stack when he felt his heart tighten and the blood in his veins run cold. He thought he was tightening his grip on the records, but instead he allowed all but the one on the top of the stack to slip out of his grip and onto the floor with a crash that sounded far louder in his ears than it should have.

"What is it?" Aubrey asked.

Jonah held the file out to her, struggling to process what he was seeing.

"It's yours."

11

Nana settled the large pot that she was carrying on the ground and wiped her hands on her pants. She looked down at her palms and saw them streaked with red dirt. Ahead of her she heard a laugh.

"That's why you should be wearing gloves."

She flashed Gannon a face, but she didn't know if he even saw her through his concentration on the planters on the table in front of him.

"You aren't wearing gloves," she pointed out.

The hybrid man didn't stop his work but held up one hand.

"Does this look like the hand of a person who frequently wears gloves?"

He flashed her a smile and went back to carefully transplanting tiny bean vine seedlings into the small pots spread across the table. Nana laughed, but in the same moment the appearance of his palm and the undersides of his fingers was horrifying. They were marked with a complex pattern of scars and callouses, the remnants of the many years that he had spent held captive by Ryan. She didn't want to know what he had gone through to give him those scars, or what any of the other hybrids had gone through. It was something that she knew that she would one day need to know, but her heart and her mind weren't ready for it yet. She would talk to them about it when she knew that things had been worked out and that she would be able to handle it. For now, she would simply put it behind her and move on, giving them the help that they desperately needed to have a life ahead of them rather than dwelling on what had been.

"Well, I left mine over on the other side of the greenhouse and by the time that I realized that I hadn't put them back on, I was already more than halfway here with that behemoth of pot and I decided I wasn't going to lug that thing all the way back over there so that I could put some gloves on to protect my hands while carrying it. I might as well just keep going because it would end up with about the same in the end."

"Except that you could have just as easily put the pot down, walked back over to your gloves, walked back, and then picked up the pot again to bring it over here."

Nana thought about this for a brief moment before feeling incredibly foolish.

"That would have been a far better plan. What would I do without you, Gannon?"

"You did just fine up until we came along," he said.

Nana started back across the greenhouse to retrieve her gloves before she could allow the emotions that she was feeling to take over. There was levity in the words, but she could still feel their impact. Of all of the people Aubrey brought to her house that night, she had connected most closely with Gannon. This massive, powerful man was something far more than just the weapon that Ryan had designed, and she was unspeakably grateful that they had rescued him from the facility. There was something truly remarkable about him and she wanted to do anything that she could to protect him and help him to discover the life that he really deserved.

He had been in her house for a few days when she noticed him show interest in the greenhouse out back. Though she didn't ask what drew him to them so much, she could tell that he wanted to see them and explore them, and she brought him with her one morning. Instantly Gannon fell in love with the plants. As the days passed, he became more and more involved with the plants, and more and more invested in the abundance of the fruits and vegetables. Nana had always seen her greenhouses as a hobby, just something to fill her time and sometimes provide her with crops that she could enjoy. In Gannon, though, she saw a purpose, a drive that brought him out before the sun rose and kept him there as long as Nana would permit.

Gannon thrived in the greenhouses. In even the short time that he had been helping her, he had brought new life and lushness to the fruits and vegetables. Though she had always prided herself in the health of her gardens and the wealth of produce that she was able to use in her kitchen at harvesttime. Immediately, however, she recognized that there was something about Gannon that went beyond just her understanding and skill with the plants. He was able to detect issues that she would never have thought of and provide solutions that saved plants she likely would have lost, and coaxed what seemed like the beginnings of a harvest more bountiful than anything that she had ever grown, but it was more than that. He was happier and more confident now than when they first met, and she could see the peace that was coming over him the longer that he spent in the greenhouse. It seemed to be soothing his soul, helping him to forget everything that happened to him during his life.

Nana had picked up her gloves and was starting back toward Gannon when movement out of the corner of her eye brought her attention out of the greenhouse to a figure walking down the sidewalk along the side of her house. A few seconds later she recognized that it was Willow, a young woman who had become a close friend of Nana's despite their age difference. It had been several weeks since she had seen her, but while she was happy to see her again, she felt suddenly nervous about her coming into the greenhouse and seeing Gannon.

There wasn't anything particularly strange or startling about Gannon. He was very tall, but times had changed since she was young. Now Earth played host to so many species that it wasn't unusual to encounter non-humans. Many young people seemed to barely even notice when they interacted with those who were different from them. As she watched Willow approach, however, she knew that it wasn't this woman's reaction to Gannon that she was concerned about. Instead it was Gannon's reaction to her. He had had such little interaction with others and it had taken him time to even trust Nana enough to talk to her without Jonah or Aubrey in the room. Nana's compulsion was to protect him just as she wanted to protect the rest of those who had come to find solace and sanctuary in her home. She wanted to guard them, to shield them from any more pain or difficulty.

In truth, though, she knew that this wasn't realistic. She couldn't expect to simply keep the hybrids and women trapped in her home for the rest of their lives. Eventually they would be healed enough that they would be ready to leave and try to create their own lives, and that meant that they were going to have to be prepared to handle interacting and spending time with people other than those in the house. Willow was probably going to be the best way to start. She rushed toward Gannon and took him gently by the elbow.

"Gannon, a friend of mine is here."

"Do Jonah and Aubrey know that you invited someone here?"

"I didn't invite her. She comes to visit sometimes. She has greenhouses, too. It's how we built our friendship. Besides, I don't need permission to have someone at my own house."

Gannon looked stung.

"I didn't mean..."

"I know," Nana said. "I just want you to remember that you are alright. Eventually you are going to have a life outside of all of this, and you are going to do just fine."

THE DOOR to the greenhouse opened and Gannon turned to see a stunning woman step inside. She looked around and then her eyes fell on Nana and she smiled. He felt stuck in place, unable to do anything but just look at her. She crossed the greenhouse toward them and Nana stepped forward to take her into a warm embrace. Nana stepped back and looked at the younger woman with a smile.

"I'm so glad to see you. It's been too long."

"I know. I'm sorry. Things have been crazy. But I wanted to stop by and see how your plants are coming along."

"It's still early yet, but I think that I'm getting a pretty good start."

The woman looked around at the plants nearby, her face registering obvious surprise.

"I would say so," she said. "These are gorgeous. How have you made them so strong already?"

"Well," Nana said, stepping back slightly and gesturing at Gannon. "That's all thanks to Gannon here. Gannon, this is Willow."

Willow turned to look at him and their eyes met. He felt a strange jump in his heartrate, but couldn't bring himself to say anything.

"Hello," Willow said.

She didn't seem put off by him, and Gannon was immediately taken by feelings that he couldn't understand. It was a draw, an attraction that he had never experienced. He had never been in a situation that would allow him to be attracted to someone and the sensation hit him hard. He didn't know anything about what he was feeling except that he wanted to be near her, to listen to her and share these moments with her in any way that he could.

"Hello," he finally said, not knowing how long had passed since she had spoken.

Willow's smile widened slightly and she exchanged glances with Nana.

"I haven't seen you around," Willow said. "How long have you known Nana?"

Gannon wasn't sure how to respond. He looked to Nana, who smiled and linked her arm with Willow's.

"Let me show you what Gannon has been able to do with my tomato plants. I wasn't expecting anything from them, especially this early in the season. They were just a couple of clippings from my plants from last year, but Gannon was able to transform them."

Willow looked at Gannon for a few seconds longer and

then allowed Nana to guide her away from him. He watched as they made their way over to a row of tomato plants that had been one of the first projects that he had taken up when Nana showed him the greenhouse. It hadn't escaped Gannon's attention that Nana had avoided answering the question of how long they had known each other, and he was sure that she wasn't going to tell Willow how they had actually met, who he was, or where he had come from, but he didn't know how he should feel about it. He had spent so much of his life anonymous and overlooked, but at the same time he didn't know how he would have explained it all to her, either. Until this moment he hadn't thought about what it would be like to encounter someone completely outside of the situation and what it would mean to talk about what he had gone through. Now he was feeling things that he never knew possible and the reality of there being more to life than captivity was suddenly sharp and detailed.

Gannon walked up to the plants and noticed Willow touching the leaves. Her fingers ran over the budding fruits and she turned to him.

"These plants are absolutely beautiful, Gannon," she said. "How do you do it?"

Gannon shrugged. He couldn't tell her the truth of why he knew so much about these plants and how to nurture them so that they would thrive and become as strong and productive as possible. Telling her that would be telling her too much. Instead he just smiled at her and reached out to break a wilting leaf off of the vine.

"It's just a passion of mine," he said. "I guess I'm good at it."

Willow walked down the row of plants and touched the growing fruit on another of them. This vine he had trained on a spiral of wire so that it could grow more densely without taking up as much space. She examined the spiral and then looked at him.

"Maybe sometime soon you can come over to my greenhouse and help me with some of my plants."

Gannon saw Nana's eyes slide over to Willow but he couldn't decipher the thoughts behind the expression. Gannon didn't know how to respond. It pleased him that she would think to ask him to do that and he knew that he wanted to spend more time with her, but he couldn't deny the nervous feeling gnawing at his belly. Going to her house to help her meant spending time interacting with someone he didn't know and who didn't know him. There had been no preparation, no lead-in that would help her to understand his perspective and no guidance to help him understand hers. He would have to figure this out as it came.

12

———

Kyven stood watching Mhavrych for several minutes without speaking. The other man was laying weapons out on the floor of the bedroom that he once slept in when he was a child. They had pushed aside all of the furniture, clearing out the center of the room and creating the image that life had moved on. That image of his childhood was broken, moved aside so that the new reality could set in.

Mhavrych had organized the weapons from his father's war room into different groups, arranging them by style and size, readying for the training that they would begin the next morning. They had only a short time to prepare all of the people who had agreed to go to Penthos by training them to use these weapons and instructing them on how to fight. Having the weapons laid out this way would make it easier to distribute them to the appropriate people and teach them effectively.

Kyven had been stunned to see Mhavrych when she walked up with Athan and his mother. He had seen this man only briefly when he had come to rescue Kyven and

Emerie on Penthos, and he had left before Kyven had even been able to thank him for what he did. The last place that he would have expected to encounter him again was on Uoria, walking out in the open with the two people who had been closest to him as he grew up. He didn't understand how he had gotten there or why, and he knew that he needed to talk to him.

"Standing there longer isn't going to make it any easier for you."

Kyven was startled by Mhavrych suddenly talking to him. The man was still arranging the weapons and had not turned to him, but it was obvious he was directing the comment at Kyven. He considered leaving the doorway, but knew that he couldn't. Instead, he took a few steps into the room.

"I didn't think that I would see you here," he said. "I didn't even know that you had any connections with Uoria."

"You didn't even know that I existed," Mhavrych pointed out.

The man's harsh demeanor was as off-putting and unexpected as it had been when he heard him speak in the chamber with Creia and Rey. Though he wouldn't have described the way that he interacted with him and Emerie when he was helping them get away from the Meldor and out of the quarry as kind or friendly, Kyven could reconcile the man who had come down into the ground and risked his own life to save his and the brooding, angry man that was now in front of him.

"You left before I was able to thank you," Kyven said.

"You didn't need to thank me."

"You saved my life and the life of my mate. I think that that more than justifies thanks. You just left too quickly for me to say anything."

"I needed to get away from there," Mhavrych said. "I didn't want to be noticed."

"Why were you there? You can't be a part of the hybrids. I know that you saved Nylek as well."

It was a stream of thoughts, what was bouncing in his mind tumbling out of his mouth without control. Mhavrych stopped and turned toward Kyven. Looking into his face brought back the horrifying memories of being trapped beneath the ground with the hot, heavy breath of the Meldor on his skin. He had been positive that he was going to die that night, that those moments were the last that he was going to have, and all he could do was try to protect Emerie. Mhavrych had been exactly what the meaning of his name stated, a miracle. Now, though, he looked like a storm and Kyven felt the chill of his presence roll down his spine.

"You're right," Mhavrych said. "I'm not one of the hybrid army. I had my reasons for being on Penthos. Reasons that mean that I need to get back there again. My reasons are my own, but I also couldn't just let you die out there without even having a chance."

Mhavrych started out of the room, but just as he passed Kyven, he turned to him again.

"Your name is Kyven," he said, not a question but a statement.

Kyven nodded.

"Yes," he said.

Mhavrych gave a single nod and continued to stare at him for a few seconds before he spoke again.

"That does make the help that I gave you matter more to me," he said.

Kyven looked back at him quizzically.

"Why?" he asked.

"When I found you in the quarry, I didn't know that you were Aegeus's son. Now that I know that, helping you is more meaningful to me. I will always be proud and honored to serve your father."

Without any further explanation, Mhavrych left the room and Kyven heard him walking toward the back of the house and the war room. He waited until he could no longer hear his footsteps before leaving the room and starting toward the house that he was sharing with Emerie. She was in the kitchen when he entered and he could smell the strong, spicy smell of one of his favorite foods from when was a child. She turned to him and smiled.

"Hi," she said.

"Hi," he answered, leaning down to kiss her. "Smells wonderful."

"Thank you. Your mom gave me the recipe yesterday. She said that you loved it when you were little."

"She always used to make it for me on special occasions. Or sometimes just because she wanted to make me feel special. That was hard growing up with Maxim."

Emerie laughed, but then she saw his face fall slightly and she tilted her head to look at him.

"What is it?" she asked. "Did something happen at your mom's house?"

Kyven drew in a breath and sat down at the table.

"Mhavrych was with Mama and Athan when I found them," he said.

Emerie looked at him strangely.

"Mhavrych?" she asked. "The man who helped us when we were in the quarry?"

Kyven nodded.

"Yes."

He accepted the cup of coffee that Emerie held out to

him and took a long sip before trying to explain the entire situation to her. He told her what had happened in the room with Creia and Rey, and then about his encounter with Mhavrych in Ellora's house. When he finished, Emerie was still standing beside the stove, stirring the food almost absently as she thought through what he had said to her.

"What do you think that he meant by he had his own reasons for being on Penthos? What could he be doing there that would also bring him here?"

"I don't know," Kyven said. "I wish that Maxim was here and that I could talk to him about all of this. He would understand."

"Would he?" Emerie asked. "Why do you think that Maxim would automatically know something that you didn't?"

"Maxim is older than me. When our father died, he was all that was left for me to look up to other than Athan. It was easier for me to transfer my trust and reliance over to Maxim rather than Athan, because he already reminded me so much of Papa. Well, they both did, but in different ways. Athan reminded me of him as a soldier and brought back memories of when he left. He was a reminder that Papa was gone and that he wasn't going to come back. Maxim reminded me of the times that we used to spend together as a family. He was a reminder of Papa's strength and how much I adored him. Even now that we are adults, I look at Maxim and I see the replacement for my father. I always assume that he knows things that I don't and that he can do things that I would never be able to do."

"That's not true, Kyven," Emerie said. "Yes, Maxim is an extraordinary leader and has proven himself to be invaluable to everything that's been happening, but I think that you are capable of so much more than you give yourself credit for."

"What do you mean?"

"Don't forget that I saw you every day that you were trapped in that meeting hall. I saw everything that you went through and the strength that you showed. Maxim wasn't there. He didn't go through that. He had his own struggles, yes, but that shouldn't discount what you went through. You were able to overcome that and move forward. Not everyone could do that. How many of those men who were there with you refused to stay with the rest of the group? How many refuse to fight alongside Pyra even though he apologized for what he did and has proven that he is devoted to all of Uoria, and not just the Denynso?"

"I just wish that I could do more. I hate that I am here and not there with him facing whatever it is that he is facing."

"There's so much that you can do here, Kyven. Soon enough we'll be back there. For now, concentrate on what you can do to make sure that everyone here is as prepared as possible for when we arrive. That is the most important thing that you can do."

"What Mhavrych said is still bothering me," he said. "Why would he mention my father? How does he know him? He looks far too young to have had any kind of relationship with Papa before he died. It just doesn't make any sense."

Emerie shook her head at him. She rested the spoon to the top of the pot and came to kneel down in front of him.

"Kyven," she said. "Don't you remember? Your father isn't dead."

The words sounded like they were coming both through her voice and through his memories, reminding him of the moment when he saw Ryan's face appear in the ship and heard that Aegeus had not died in that final battle the way that they all assumed he had. It had been such an incredible revelation, something that he never could have imagined, and it was still difficult for him to truly accept. Hearing it, though, seemed to reinforce him, strengthening him as he felt the boost of his father's presence and the hope that he would soon see him again, but also with the fire in his belly that came from knowing all of the pain that his family had gone through since he was a child was falsified, crafted by Ryan while his father suffered.

"I need to find Mhavrych," he said.

"Why?" Emerie asked.

"My father knows and trusts him. I'm going to have to do the same if I'm going to have the best chances of helping bring all of this to a resolution."

"Do you really think that there is a resolution waiting on Penthos?" Emerie asked.

"What do you mean?" Kyven asked.

"This all seems so big, so much more than just Nyx 23 and the Order. Do you really think that this war will end it?"

"I don't know," Kyven admitted. "I don't know what's going to happen. All I do know is that I have to try. All of us have to try. We lost so much and there is so much more that we could lose. I can't let that happen."

Kyven stood and walked over to Emerie, opening his arms to her. She stepped into them and he wrapped his arms tightly around her, leaning down to rest his chin on the top of her head so that he could envelope her in him as much as possible.

"I love you," he said. "I would go through all of this again if I knew that it would bring me back to you. There's nothing that I wouldn't do, nothing that I wouldn't try, if it meant protecting you and ensuring that we will be together."

He felt her arms tighten around his waist and she nuzzled her face into his chest.

"I love you, too," she said. "I never believed that I would be able to find someone to love again. When we crashed, I thought that any joy that I might have ever had in my life was gone. I was going to live the rest of my life alone and just live out my days in the settlement, waiting for them to be over. Then I found you." She leaned back so that she could look up at him. "I believe that there is a part of my heart that was always waiting for you and no matter what I had to go through to get here, I will be forever grateful that the suffering that I endured brought me to your arms. Whatever else we have to face, we are going to face it together, and I know that we will have a beautiful life together when this is all through."

Their mouths met and Kyven let his eyes close, giving himself over to the kiss so that he could pretend, if only for those few moments, that it was already finished and they were living the beautiful life that existed in Emerie's mind.

13

TO BE CONTINUED...

Maxim found Pyra standing at the entrance to the compound two nights later and approached him carefully. The massive Denynso warrior stared out past the throw of the flames from the torches positioned along the inside of the stone wall into the darkness of the desert beyond. They hadn't heard the drums since the battle and around them the energy of the compound was beginning to lose its frenetic intensity as everyone began to settle, quieting as they gathered and conserved their energy for whatever was coming next.

"Pyra?"

Pyra looked over at Maxim.

"Yes, Maxim? Is something wrong?"

"No," Maxim said quickly, wanting to diffuse the anxiety and temper that were still strong inside Pyra. "Everything's fine. I just wanted to thank you."

"Thank me?" Pyra asked. "For what?"

"For what you did for my father. He told me about everything that you did to help him on Earth. I can't tell you how much I appreciate it all. You ensured that I got my father back."

"You're welcome, Maxim. I'm happy that we were able to bring him here to you."

Though he was accepting Maxim's thanks and genuinely did seem glad about the near-miraculous reunion that he had in part facilitated, Pyra's face was drawn and there was concern in his voice.

"What is it, Pyra?" he asked. "Did you hear the drums?"

"No," Pyra said. "It's been silent since the battle."

"Is it something else?"

Pyra looked out over the sand again.

"I'm worried about the people that we left behind in the ship. I think that we need to go back for them."

Maxim felt confused. He shook his head slightly.

"I thought that your crew transferred the other injured and the pregnant women onto the bigger ship because they would be safer there. Don't they have everything that they need to sustain them, at least for a while if not until we are able to head back to Uoria?"

"We originally brought them to the main ship because we thought that it would be safer for them to remain there rather than trying to transfer them across the planet, especially since we didn't know where to find you. They have enough supplies to keep them going, but I don't feel confident that they are safe any longer."

"Why?" Maxim asked.

"Now that we've had a battle with the hybrids and I've seen what they are capable of and their ruthlessness, I feel like making that decision put them in serious danger. Leaving them in the ship out in the desert without any of the warriors or anyone to watch over them and help them if there is an ambush makes them far too vulnerable. Nearly all of those who are still there are already severely injured or pregnant. They aren't able to take care of themselves or protect themselves as we would be. Though there are still some weapons aboard, they are far from prepared to fight. What would happen if the hybrids decided to try to invade the ship? They would have no way of keeping them out unless the pilot has activated the defense shields. Even then, there's a chance that the hybrid army has access to weapons that could completely destroy the ship and everyone on it. We need to go back for them and bring them here to the compound where they will be safer. The injured have had enough opportunity to undergo more treatments so they should be stronger and better able to handle the journey. Once we get them here, Ciyrs, Elianna, and Eden can administer healings. They'll be able to keep an eye on the pregnant women as well. There are some of them who should be delivering fairly soon."

Maxim nodded.

"I think you're right," he said. "They will be safer if they are here with people who can help them. What if they refuse to come or are too afraid?"

"We're just going to have to convince them," Pyra said. "They have already gone through far more difficult and dangerous situations than this. If they can survive what Ryan put them through, then they can face crossing the desert. They will need as many of us with them as possible."

"I'll go with you," Maxim agreed. "I'm sure that my father will as well."

Pyra shook his head.

"No, Maxim," he said. "Aegeus needs to stay here."

"Why?" Pyra asked. "He got through the battle unscathed. I am more wounded than he is. He is whole and strong again. He'll be able to help protect them."

"Aegeus escaped from Ryan," Pyra said. "After so many years, he was able to get out of Ryan's control and has fought against the hybrids. The Valdicians are going to want to bring him back to Earth and present him to Ryan for whatever punishment he wants to administer. Aegeus is at far more risk than any of the rest of us, even the hybrids. They are dispensable. He knows that he can easily replace them. Not Aegeus. Even Ryan can't replace Aegeus."

"Because he doesn't have other Mikana?" Maxim asked. "He doesn't have all of the Klimnu DNA that he wants for his experiments and needs to recapture him so that he can transform him again?"

"No," Pyra said. "Because he's who he is. There is much about your father that you don't know, Maxim. Ryan will do anything it takes to get his hands on him again."

"How are we going to transfer them all?" Maxim asked. "Even without my father with us, we're going to be targeted by the army. They've been quiet since the battle, but they aren't going to stay that way. They are planning something. Crossing the desert will make all of us vulnerable and exposed, and we need to be as prepared as we can to get there and get back here to the compound."

"You're right," Pyra said.

"About what?" Maxim asked.

"The hybrids. They've been quiet. They haven't attacked in two days. They haven't even warned with their drums. The battle affected them a lot more than they thought that it was going to. It wasn't just us, though."

"The Meldor," Maxim said. "They fell apart when they saw the Meldor."

"We should go talk to Severine. She knows more about that animal than any of us, and might be able to tell us why all of the hybrids reacted the way that they did."

"We may be able to utilize the Meldor in some way during the transfer. It could help."

Pyra nodded.

"We'll talk to her in the morning," he agreed. "Go get some sleep. Your guard shift is in a few hours."

SEVERINE LOOKED out at the two men in surprise. They stood outside the door of the barn, looking at her hopefully, asking if they could come inside to talk to her about the Meldor. She didn't know how to respond. Neither man had responded well to the animal when they saw it during the battle and in the times that they saw it in the compound since. Part of her worried that they were trying to gain access to it so that they could hurt it in some way, and she felt her defenses sparking as she searched their faces.

"Can we come in?" Maxim asked again.

Severine nodded and stepped back to allow the two men to come into the barn with her. They both paused when they realized that the Meldor was not in a stall, but roaming free within the building. It's tremendous size seemed amplified by the constraints of the building, but it was peaceful and calm. In just the short time since she and Rilex had rescued the animal from its underground prison it had become accustomed to her and she could feel that they were forming a bond.

"What is it that I can do for the two of you?" Severine asked, keeping her body positioned purposely between the men and the Meldor.

Maxim and Pyra exchanged glances and then Maxim stepped slightly toward her.

"We need your help," he said.

Severine was somewhat startled by the admission. It felt like a major step that these two men were coming to her asking for help and she felt empowered knowing that there was something that they felt she had to offer to the war. At the same time, she wished that Rilex was there with her. She still wasn't accustomed to spending time with people without him and she felt unsure of herself as she faced Maxim and Pyra. She straightened her spine, trying to reassure herself that she could handle this one her own. As much as she was committed to sharing her life with Rilex, that didn't mean that they would be together at every moment. There would be more and more times like this when she was on her own with others and she would need to be able to manage it comfortably.

"What can I do for you?" she asked.

"It is more what...that...can do," Pyra said, gesturing behind her.

"The Meldor?" Severine said, part question, part insistence that he refer to the animal as what it was.

"Yes," Maxim said. He looked at the animal and then back at Severine. "Do you know if it's..." his voice trailed off.

"It's male," Severine said.

Maxim nodded.

"We think that he could be extremely helpful for us, but we don't understand him the way that you do."

"What do you want from him?" Severine asked suspiciously.

"We want to go back to the ship and bring the injured and the women back here to the compound so that they can be safer," Pyra said. "We think that the Meldor could be helpful in that transition."

"We all saw how the hybrids reacted to him when you rode him into battle," Maxim said. "It was obvious that they were afraid of it. That could be instrumental in getting us across the desert to the ship and then back with the rest."

"The Others," Severine said, using the word that she had adopted for herself. "They are the Others. All of us who don't fit into one of your species or who were used in the experiments are."

The men nodded and she could see the respect in their eyes.

"Do you think that he could help?" Pyra asked.

"I think that having him with you could be helpful in keeping the hybrid army at bay, at least more than they would be if you just tried to go on your own."

"I think that we should go tonight," Pyra said. "If we go when they might be sleeping, they will be tired. Those who were in the battle might still be recovering from that."

Severine shook her head.

"No," she said. "That won't matter. We should wait and go tomorrow morning."

"Why?" Maxim asked.

"The hybrids don't care about being tired. They have been trained to the point that they will literally fight until they die from exhaustion. No level of tiredness or recovery from a battle will keep them from fighting if that is what they are called to do. Being tired doesn't have any meaning to them. Their fear of the Meldor, though, does."

"I don't understand," Pyra said.

"I've never seen any of the hybrids react to anything the way that they did to this animal when they saw it." She walked up to the side of the Meldor and gently patted his side. She had been working on his coat with a brush and many of the mats were gone, revealing just how thick and beautiful the fur really was. "In my training, the Meldor was something to be wary of, but not something to fear. They've been taught something about this animal that is terrifying them and causing them to break ranks and leave a battle, which is never something that they would do."

"But why do you think that we should go during the day? Wouldn't we be more concealed if we went at night?"

"You might be more concealed," Severine said, "but so will the hybrid army. The Meldor will be most effective during the day. The hybrids have been taught that he will only come out in the dark, that he can't tolerate the light. When I removed his collar, though, I ensured that he was able to go out in the light without any consequences. They hybrids now know that we have the Meldor and that it is out of the tunnels. They will expect it to be used. But they will expect that it will only come out at night. If they see you out with him during the day it will have a tremendous impact on them."

"Why?" Maxim asked.

"The army has been trained since the time that they were old enough to understand anything around them to believe that things are the way that they are. Period. There is no deviation, there is no option. They live in a world where all they know is what Ryan and the Valdicians have told them, and they structure their entire existences around those realities. If they see the Meldor out during the day it will throw them completely off balance. They will be confused and not know what to think. Seeing that animal coming toward them out in the full light of the day will force them to recognize that everything is not necessarily as it seems or as they have been told, and that there are other options and other possibilities."

"What will that do?" Pyra asked.

"It could do two things," Severine told him. "It could snap them out of the fog of control that Ryan has them under and let them see that the life that they have is theirs and they can do with it as they please. Or it could make it so that they aren't sure of anything any longer and don't know what they are supposed to do next. Whichever way, it will buy you some time and make it easier for you to get to the ship or back here. The Meldor will also be extremely beneficial if any of those who are still on the ship are still too injured to handle the entirety of the journey. You can place them up on his back and he will be able to transport them safely."

"Will you come along with us?" Maxim asked. "He seems to trust you and you'll be able to guide him properly."

Severine hesitated. She wasn't sure if she could face the idea of crossing the desert without more of the warriors or other soldiers with her. The Meldor nudged her as if to reassure her and she nodded.

"Yes," she said. "I'll go with you."

www.ingramcontent.com/pod-product-compliance
Lightning Source LLC
Chambersburg PA
CBHW032036180726
48284CB00008B/2616